A Touch

morbid

LEAH CLIFFORD

Greenwillow Books
An Imprint of HarperCollins*Publishers*

To my parents, Noreen and Scot Clifford—I lucked out being your kid

A Touch Morbid
Copyright © 2012 by Leah Clifford

The text of this book is set in 11-point Ehrhardt MT.
Book design by Paul Zakris

Library of Congress Cataloging-in-Publication Data
Clifford, Leah.
A touch morbid / Leah Clifford.
p. cm.
"Greenwillow Books."
Summary: Eden, a powerful Sider caught between life and death, has difficult choices to make as the war between Heaven and Hell rages on, endangering Gabriel, Kristen, and Az, and the poison Eden refuses to spread to mortals slowly builds inside her.
ISBN 978-0-06-200502-1 (trade bdg.)
[1. Future life—Fiction. 2. Angels—Fiction. 3. Demonology—Fiction.
4. Dead—Fiction.] I. Title.
PZ7.C622148Tom 2012   [Fic]—dc23   2011029231

12 13 14 15 16 LP/RRDH 10 9 8 7 6 5 4 3 2 1
First Edition

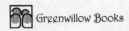
Greenwillow Books

Her feet go down to death;
her steps take hold on hell.

—PROVERBS 5:5

CHAPTER 1

When the kitten broke out of the shadows in front of Gabe, he'd thought it was another rat until he heard the pathetic mewling. It darted for his leg, fearlessly sliding against the stained jeans Gabe wore. He reached down without thinking, pinched the black fur of its scruff, and lifted it.

The kitten dangled, a tight casing of fur stretched over bones. It let out another pitiful cry. Gabe cupped his hand and plopped the tiny back end of the kitten into it.

"Helpless little thing, aren't you?" he said quietly. It twitched its bent whiskers. Gabe squatted, resting on his boot heels. Behind his ribs, the evil took hold, liquid nitrogen spreading frost down his arms. He could feel it, like ice crystals forming under his skin. It crept into his fingers.

A trickle of shame slid between his shoulder blades, but he knew the feeling wouldn't win. *One flick of the wrist.* A slight twist and he would feel much better.

"I'll be so quick." Gabe slid his hand down the kitten's neck, the sharp spine below the surface grating against his palm.

Under his fingers, the damaged thing seemed to rumble suddenly to life. He felt it even through the icy numbness.

"Are you purring?" he asked it. It bumped a pink nose into his palm, rattling with pleasure.

He could feed it. The thought popped into his head. A whole new possibility suddenly there. A hollow ache rippled through him, his fingers warming, the coldness receding.

The kitten's matted tail curled around his wrist.

"You," he told it, "are making a mistake. You should run. This won't end well." Still, he stood with a wince, cradling the kitten.

He carried the thing back home, to the random apartment. The kitten mewed again as he climbed to the security door. "Almost there."

Inside, the decrepit elevator groaned as it rose, really a gated cage on cords. Gabe kept his fingers clear of the metal until it came to a stop. He juggled the kitten and eased the grate open. The carpet in the hallway was beyond threadbare, stained and cigarette burned. A light flickered dully from down near the stairwell.

The kitten was still and silent in his arm as he unlocked the door. Clicking the light on, he unzipped his coat.

"Mi casa es su casa," he said, dropping the kitten to the gouged hardwood. It sniffed curiously, then sat looking up at him as if waiting.

Gabe squeezed his hands into fists.

"It'll pass," he mumbled, more to himself than to the furry creature below. "I can learn to control this, right? Not so hard." The last words came out more a question than anything else.

The kitten poked warily around the efficiency.

"I can resist. This time will be different," Gabe said, wandering to the kitchen. The refrigerator was nearly bare—a few ancient take-out boxes he was afraid to open, and a slew of lunch meat containers close to expiring. He pulled the freshest one out, snapped it open, and dropped a hunk of shaved turkey to the tiles. The kitten pounced, sucking the meat down in airy gulps. Gabe tossed the rest of the package on the floor and licked his fingers.

He let out a slow breath, wishing there was a couch to flop onto, a TV to channel surf for distractions.

The mattress in the corner lay atop a box spring, but the bed had no frame. He slunk onto it, listening to the kitten chomp down the last bits of turkey.

In the beginning, the first days after he'd spoken his sins aloud and become one of the Fallen, his memories were murky. He remembered little of the first week, and something deep inside wasn't sure he wanted that to change. When he had snapped out of his haze, he'd found a card in his pocket, folded up tight, curled around a key. Scrawled in his own handwriting was a note. *You look great in black,* it had said, *but make sure it's a temporary trend. Never good for more than a season. Go here. Fight the urges. Remember what Az said.* The address to the apartment had been below.

No one had bothered him about rent. There had been a stocked pantry, a few thousand dollars rolled up and tucked into the medicine cabinet. Things had come back to him in the quiet darkness, slowly at first and then more frequently as time passed. A name, out-of-focus faces, best forgotten for their safety. But he still had no idea what the note meant. No idea what Az had said or what he was supposed to be doing.

A week passed. Then another. Nights in Polaroid snapshots. A dark club. Back rooms. Offers. He led the mortals astray, feasted on the hatred in their eyes when he turned them down. Left them wicked and unwanted.

Most times.

Lately, he'd locked himself in. Prayed to wake up alone and in his own bed. He drifted off, hoping this was one of those nights.

Kristen. Gabe slammed against the floor. His eyes darted around the shell of the apartment even as he shielded them from the sunlight slanting in through the blinds, trying to find the person who'd spoken. The room was empty.

"Kristen?" Her name broke on his lips. Dust sparkled through the light.

He curled his legs underneath him on the hard floor.

The apartment was so cold. He forced himself up and to the thermostat. The heat was on, turned up to seventy-eight. He pressed the button, the numbers rising, rising, but his mind caught hold of something else. A flicker of warmth inside himself.

"She's alone," he said to the empty room, his eyes focused beyond the cracked paint on the wall, the yellowed stain reaching down from the ceiling. "'With all the old nocturnal smells that cross and cross across her brain.'"

He could see her, the vision of her strengthening as the words leaked from him. Her alone and sick, two years ago. Dark hair in long tangled waves, desperate eyes. She'd been so damaged before he'd healed her. She'd been the first Sider he'd talked to and had told him what little she knew of her kind. They'd helped each other, their friendship growing strong. He'd been the only person she'd trusted.

And what's become of you without me? he thought. Her lips moved in mute, his name trembling across them.

"Kristen," he whispered again, and the spell broke.

Gabe closed his eyes. No. It was best not to think of those who used to consider him a friend. Kristen, Az, Eden. He was too dangerous, someone to keep locked in and hidden away where he couldn't hurt anyone.

A draft slid over his shoulders. He followed it across the floor to the other side of the room and swore softly. When he sighed, he could see his breath.

Sometime in the night, he'd awoken. The window was open.

The kitten was gone.

CHAPTER 2

Kristen knew the warning signs, knew to call Gabe when the thin whispers started. The static of white noise came next, when the shadows started to follow her instead of staying pinned down in the darkness. She'd called. Ninety-seven times she'd called Gabriel over the past month.

"Please," she whispered, hope fluttering in her chest as the call connected. The ribbons of her red ballet flats wrapped around her legs, cutting into her calves. She bounced lightly anyway, waiting through the ring-back tone—some club mix that Gabe had set up ages ago.

When his voice mail picked up, she stretched impatiently onto her toes, relishing the tightening pinch before she dropped and the ribbons loosened.

Kristen closed her eyes, exhaustion dragging down her shoulders. At least there, on the recording, she could still hear him, could take comfort from his voice.

Soon his voice wouldn't be enough.

You have other options.

"None I'd ever consider," she whispered to her reflection. "Stop overreacting."

Why are you acting as if Gabriel's the only one who can help you?

Part of her wondered if he was there, ignoring the calls.

There was silence on the line. Her mind had drifted.

"Hello, Ghost," she said, wondering how much dead air the recording captured before she spoke, if her earlier words were trapped there for him to hear. Embarrassment washed over her, but if he heard her talking to herself, maybe he'd forgive her and come back. "This is..." She hesitated. "Life." Sighing, she gave in and let the plea come, all she'd really needed or wanted to say. "Come back to me, Gabriel. I'm not doing well. You promised."

She hung up, dropping into the chair in front of her vanity, met her own eyes in the mirror. She kept the cell in her hand. If he'd been close and only missed the call . . .

The phone stayed silent.

You should have apologized. She rubbed a finger underneath her eyes, but the black smudges there had nothing to do with makeup, everything to do with Gabriel's absence. He'd saved her two years ago when she'd been lost to the world and out of her mind, living in an abandoned shack of a chapel at the back of a cemetery. He'd culled the schizophrenia, brought her back to herself. But he could never get it all, could never stop the roots of what was left from spreading like ivy. And so she and Gabriel had traded—her knowledge of the Suiciders for his skills at stripping the disease from her brain every few weeks. They'd learned to trust each other. Kristen depended on him. He'd promised her he'd be there, never let her get so sick again.

And then came Eden, Kristen thought bitterly.

Below her, across the lacquered surface, bottles of nail polish were lined up according to color. She put them in order from dark to light, then switched tactics, going by the level of polish left. The patterns were wrong. All of them.

He hates you; that's why he's gone.

Her fingers shifted the bottles like notes on a musical staff. Was the pattern supposed to be a song? If so, she could find the right cadence and things would be better.

The tics, needing to find order, would only worsen. Usually she fought the urge; today though, she gave in to the indulgence. A few weeks ago, Eden and Gabriel had shown up on her doorstep. Lucifer had stolen Az away, was trying to sway him to Fall. They'd made plans for a rescue—she, Gabe, and Eden—but then Eden had gone early and alone. Kristen had let her go.

Gabe had been sleeping when Eden left before dawn, but Kristen had caught her, could have stopped her.

Instead she'd dosed her up with Touch, given her all the strength she'd had and a head start.

And you said nothing. You know what Luke is capable of and you sent Eden to face him alone. Because of you, Gabriel could have lost her and Az to the Fallen. No wonder he won't speak to you, the voice berated.

When Gabe awoke, she'd expected anger, yelling, but the wrath in him, the fury blazing red in his eyes, had caught her off guard.

She lifted her eyes to the mirror and swore she caught a flash of exposed bone on her jaw. For a moment she almost felt as if her glamour shifted out of place, the dirty hidden side of herself showing. Despite being undead, she looked normal enough as long as the glamour stayed; only the touch of another Sider could drop it. Since she was alone in her room, that left two possibilities. Kristen studied herself. Had the vision been the first flicker of a hallucination or merely a trick of the light?

"It was the light," she reassured herself. "Gabriel *will* come back."

And if he doesn't?

"He only needs time."

You betrayed him. Betrayed the trust of the only person you dared call a friend. You took him for granted and now he's gone. Guilt dropped her eyes.

The last bottle of nail polish lay on its side. She spun it

in a lazy circle, the maroon color a shade too dark to be the C minor she needed to finish the song. Kristen hummed the tune softly.

It was only then that she recognized the melody, the musician who'd written it.

"Luke," she whispered.

He'd help you. Go to him.

"Never," she spat at the mirror. "Luke is not an option."

Yet. The lips of her reflection twisted up in a cruel smile.

"No!" Kristen thrust her hands out, the bottles slamming against the mirror and tumbling to the floor as she dropped her head onto her arms. "Damn it, Gabriel, where are you?"

She concentrated on the dull roar of her blood pounding through her eardrums, using the steady arterial rhythms to calm herself. She waited for voices caught in the white noise, but only heard her heartbeat.

Behind her, a throat cleared. She didn't need to glance up to know Sebastian stood at the threshold. "Everything—"

"Everything is fine," she insisted, cutting him off as she lifted her head. Sebastian regarded her, his brown eyes uncertain. Worry creased his forehead. He'd been her Second, at her side before her crew of Siders had grown to the twenty or so the house now held. Sebastian, who she knew would defend her to the death, who'd been her consort when she'd needed comfort. Her most trusted ally aside from Gabriel. Even he knew nothing of her illness. The thing Gabe had tried so hard to fix, but only managed to dull, wasn't something she would ever speak of aloud to him, no matter what he suspected. She couldn't bear the thought of him seeing her as weak. "Everything is fine."

"You're not." Sebastian stood, arms crossed, waiting, as if she'd suddenly break and confide in him. "What happened?" he asked, gesturing to the mess. He moved closer, working a fingernail into a chip missing from the corner of the mirror.

"I bumped my knee and nearly tipped the damned thing over. It's fine. I'll clean it later." She tried to work up a smile, but couldn't.

"You seem rattled." From the look on Sebastian's face, he knew the thin line he tread. He'd mastered hovering between asking too much or too little, smart enough not to force explanations for her behavior. "Should I be concerned?"

"Currently? No." She stood and pushed past him, out of the room and heading down the hall.

Sebastian followed wordlessly until she passed by the staircase and into the left wing. "Maybe it'd be better if you came straight downstairs today?"

Kristen didn't slow her steps, and Sebastian hesitated. The left wing frightened him. Frightened everyone but her, because of what it held behind its locked doors. From behind her, she heard Sebastian's hard sigh, his footsteps retreating down the staircase.

Everyone knew the rumor. The punishment for stepping out of line, standing against Kristen in any way.

Siders had to pass Touch to mortals. If they weren't able to pass it, the Touch built in them until they became overwhelmed, buried under their most terrible thoughts.

Every Sider in her home, as well as most in the other boroughs, gossiped about how she kept misbehavers locked in darkened rooms, forced them to build Touch until they lost their minds, begged to pass it to her. She let them sometimes, loading up on Touch until her tolerance built. Until she could hold more than the other Siders. In the past, when Gabe had been tied up, she'd dumped the excess Touch to clear her mind. Losing a massive amount at once would help her hang on to her sanity for a few more days.

Kristen made her way down the hall. The first rooms were occupied by normal Siders, the doors closed. They no doubt heard her. They hid more and more lately.

Screamers. The name was whispered in dark corners.

A fine line separated "charismatic leader" from "violent psychopath." Kristen kept herself somewhere in the gray area between the two—cruel when necessary, fair to the Siders under her roof who behaved. If they kept to the rules, a docile little flock, she gave them food and shelter, even the illusion of safety.

Kristen had done what she could to separate the territories, drum up hostilities that had no basis in reality. She'd banded her Siders together—threats kept them vigilant and loyal. Teaching her Siders to fear others made them more dependent on her. They thought the other leaders, Madeline in Queens, or even Eden in Manhattan, were plotting against them. Only the territory leaders knew the true danger was from the angels.

When she reached the last door, Kristen slipped the key from the pocket of her dress. On the bed sat a boy, his eyes glazed. She gave him a once-over. Frailty made him appear childish.

She closed the door behind her. Her insides hummed, eager for the release of the Touch built up inside her. Kristen sat beside him and leaned forward. The Screamer didn't move.

Her lips tingled when they made contact with his. She felt Touch release from deep inside her, pulled up as if on a string. A sigh slipped out before she cut it off, rocked back, her lips still parted. A split second of confusion drifted across the boy's face before the look sharpened to terror.

"No!" He shot off the bed, scrambling for the door,

but Kristen snatched at his ankle, tumbling him to the floor. He wrapped his arm across his stomach, curling into a ball. "I have to get rid of it! You have to let me out of here!"

She stumbled past him, trembling.

"I'm sorry. There's no other way." Kristen closed the door, locked it. His high-pitched wail made her wince. She forced her eyes open, steadying herself with a hand on the wall.

She'd given every bit of her Touch to the boy, and her head felt clearer. The time he'd bought her wouldn't be long. Soon there'd be nothing to stave off the madness.

The Screamers weren't a rumor, but no one knew the truth. They were ballast.

For a sinking ship, she thought miserably.

CHAPTER 3

The rich coffee smell wasn't enough to keep Jarrod alert. He tried to follow Zach's orders, but already a customer had screamed at him when he used nonfat milk instead of regular. Another had walked out when he'd taken too long. Zach moved around him, splashing together concoctions for the Milton's regulars before they even spit out their orders.

Jarrod rolled his shoulders. *Gotta do better,* he thought. He'd only started the job a few days ago. It'd taken him almost three weeks to heal from his fall. Rooftop swan dives were officially off his Things To Do list.

"Eden coming by today?" Zach asked, twisting to fill another paper cup.

"Not sure. Maybe. Tomorrow probably."

Zach moved in front of Jarrod, pausing enough to catch his attention. "She okay?"

Zach hadn't been told why Adam suddenly wasn't

with their crew anymore. The one time it was brought up, Jarrod's discomfort left Zach assuming there'd been a nasty breakup between Eden and Adam.

"Sure," Jarrod said, already knowing his answer came too quick to be believable. "She's got the new boyfriend so they've been holed up."

"Right." Zach frowned. "Well, tell her I miss her face."

"I'll pass it on." Jarrod took a second to strip off his dirty gloves and throw on a new pair.

"How about you? You seem off today."

Jarrod shrugged. He'd known Zach awhile now. Granted, he'd been on the other side of the counter before, a customer, not an employee. Still, if he was that easy to read, Jarrod needed to get better at hiding his worry. "Just tired. I'm sorry."

He'd spent last night out with Eden, scouring block after block, alleys and cafes and dark corners, searching for any sign of Gabe. Too many hours of rushing adrenaline. The three hours of sleep he'd gotten left him feeling drugged, disoriented. The shuffling approach of another customer brought him back to the counter.

"What can I get you?" he asked. When there was no answer, he glanced up. The girl at the counter stared at his hands. He waved one in front of her. "Order?"

"Oh," she said, as if suddenly realizing there was a

line behind her. Her eyes jumped to the menu. "Surprise me with something."

"You got it." He turned, throwing together a mix of flavors and steamed milk. He tossed some whipped cream on top and slid the cup across the counter as he took her twenty-dollar bill. When he dropped the change into her hand, she whimpered.

He froze instinctively, but he knew he hadn't passed her Touch. His gloves were fresh, and he hadn't made contact. Even if he had, she wouldn't have felt it for hours still. He eyed the girl. She stared back, her teeth digging into a chapped lip. A few minute cracks started to seep maroon. The girl didn't seem to care at all.

"We good here?" he asked slowly. She wandered off to a table without responding.

Jarrod watched her, unsure if he should mention her to Zach. If the girl was a regular, maybe he knew something about her, something that would account for her bizarre reaction to his hands. Normal customers didn't get all wigged out when he handed them their change. But she didn't act like a Sider, either.

Something familiar about her struck him. Something . . . The color drained from his face. Something Libby.

The girl reminded him of Libby. Jarrod moved aside as Zach rang up the next customer, studying the girl around a display of overpriced tea bags. Libby, who'd infiltrated their crew and betrayed them to Luke. She'd been able to kill Siders the same way Eden could, had killed James before they'd known what she was and taken out Adam on the roof.

Eden had turned Libby to ash in his arms. He knew this girl wasn't her. Still, the first night Libby'd found their crew, when she'd been amping up the "cheerleader in distress" act— this girl looked like that, like she was in trouble. Except something in her eyes, that split lip, made him believe she wasn't acting. She looked like she'd had a rough night. A rough year.

She looked like she needed help.

"Well, look who decided to grace us with her presence," Zach said.

Jarrod's attention whipped to the counter. Eden smirked at him from the other side, Az behind her.

"I told Zach I didn't know if you'd be in today. Needed a caffeine fix, eh?"

Unless they'd found Gabe. He gave Eden a closer look. "Anything new?"

"You only left a little bit ago. Our lives aren't that exciting." Jarrod caught the sarcasm and rolled his eyes. "Think you can handle making me something?" Eden asked, changing the subject.

He turned to grab a cup, but Zach was already there.

"She's easy. Always the same and she leaves a kick-ass tip," Zach said, setting a large coffee cup in front of Eden. "Best kind of customer." He leaned closer to Eden and wiped at her cheek with a gloved hand. She jerked away, her palm rising to her face. "Sorry, you had something black on you."

She scooted back, into Az. "What was it?"

"A fuzz or something," Zach said. He tilted his chin up at Az. "Want anything?"

He stared at the menu board for a second before shrugging. "I don't know, surprise me."

Jarrod couldn't help but glance in the direction the girl had gone. "Nobody'll make a decision today."

From a table far back in the corner, the girl watched him. No. She focused slightly in front of him. On Eden. Jarrod nodded in the girl's direction. "You know her?" he asked Eden.

Eden and Az turned. The girl didn't look away.

Az slipped his arm around Eden's waist. "She sure seems interested."

Jarrod tapped the order into the cash register and grabbed the bill Eden held out. "I rang her out. She seemed bizarre," he said as he made change.

"Like bizarre how, Jarrod?" Eden leaned on the counter, gauging his reaction.

Jarrod shrugged. "Jumpy around my hands."

"You didn't—" Eden paled, glancing down, and waved away her change, the motion a double meaning.

"Of course not," Jarrod cut her off. He tilted his head at the girl. "But there's something off about her."

Eden turned to Az. "Any thoughts?" Jarrod heard what she'd really asked Az: Was it the Bound? The Fallen? He fought to keep the fear off his face. Zach knew nothing of Upstairs or Downstairs, any angels, and for now it was best that it stay that way. Az shook his head, and Jarrod released a breath he hadn't realized he held.

"I'll keep an eye on her," Jarrod said. He grabbed a cup, filled it for Az, and handed it over.

"Let me know. Az and I are going to head to the Bronx." Eden paused. "Kristen needs to know about Gabe. The truth. We can use her help looking for him."

Jarrod followed her down the counter as she moved toward the door. If she was going to Kristen, Eden must be way more spent than she let on. "You want to wait until I get off?"

They hadn't told Kristen about Gabe's Fall. He wasn't sure exactly what Eden *had* told her about what happened that morning. It hadn't mattered to him. It wasn't like Kristen was a friend of theirs.

Eden shook her head. "No, we've got it." Before they went outside, Eden turned back. Even from the counter, Jarrod saw the way she hesitated before her eyes sparked with defiance. Whatever she was about to say, he wasn't going to like it. "Az and I are going out later tonight. Just us."

Jarrod grabbed a rag from the counter, swiped angrily. Their date night thing seemed an unnecessary chance, though he couldn't really be too pissed since they all searched for Gabe every night. The problem was how exhausted Eden looked. She was pushing herself too hard. She'd done it before, when she'd been killing the Siders and the buildup of Touch had messed her up. Now she was testing her limits again. And like last time, it fell on Jarrod to play the asshole. "Shouldn't you rest or something? I thought the point of telling Kristen was getting backup. You look like shit, Eden."

Eden's glare burned into him as Az strode back to the counter.

"Listen, don't be like this," Az said, his voice cool, low enough not to carry to Eden. "We've all been through hell, man. But that girl," he pointed back to Eden, "deserves something happy. One night, Jarrod. She needs it. I need it." Az shifted closer to be sure Jarrod caught his meaning.

Jarrod wiped down the espresso machine, focusing on it so he wouldn't give away his anger. He didn't trust Az. Not when at any moment he could snap. He'd seen what the Fallen could do. "If you're having trouble not Falling, you should have told us."

"And now I have." Az stepped back from the counter. "We won't be too late. We'll both have phones." He swung the door open for Eden.

"Jarrod!" Eden's eyes flicked to the back of the coffee shop. "Be careful."

When he turned, the strange girl raised a hand, her fingers twitching in a half wave. Jarrod didn't look away until she faltered, going back to her coffee. Whatever trouble she was in, he didn't want any part of it.

CHAPTER 4

The last time Eden had ridden the train to Kristen's, Gabe had been with her. They'd been going to Kristen for help getting Az back from Luke. She felt as hopeless now as she did then. At least this time, there would be no death. No Falling.

Eden tried to lose herself in the rhythm of the train, but the familiar guilt rolled over her. Now it was Az beside her, and Kristen would be the one devastated.

They'd lied to Kristen.

No, Eden thought, I *lied to her.* Minutes after Luke had stumbled away that morning, Kristen had called. Eden hardly remembered the call, only the frantic tone of Kristen's voice. Rapid-fire questions. *What happened? Did Az Fall?* Eden had done her best to get the details out as fast as possible, her attention on Jarrod, who had still been so broken, and Az, barely holding out against the Fall. *Didn't Gabriel find you?* Kristen had asked. It was only then that Eden realized she'd left out everything about Gabe. *He wasn't very pleased with me when he left. Because of you*, Kristen had said, something off in her voice. Eden had latched on to the idea. *He needs some time to cool down, Kristen. Give it a few days.*

One simple lie. She should have told Kristen what had really happened. *It's all my fault*, Eden thought. *Gabe's Fall, everything. All because of me.*

Eden's gaze wandered to Az. Even the thought of the Fallen was enough to light fire to her rage at seeing him hurt, the terror of almost losing him. A light scar on his cheek was faded but still visible. The memory of the shears so close to his face, already glistening with his blood, fought to the forefront of her mind. *He's still here*, she reassured herself.

She gave Az's hand a squeeze.

"You okay?" he asked.

She nodded, then reconsidered. They'd made a pact. No secrets between them, no lies. "Actually, not really."

"Too many people?"

"It's not that," she said. The mortals around her on the train weren't as distracting as the Siders that still camped out on her stairs every morning. Without the constant excess Touch she absorbed at each Sider's death, being in public wasn't as tempting as she'd thought it'd be. The cold snap that had rolled in this morning had helped, since the mortals left little skin exposed.

Actually, she realized suddenly, she hadn't spread Touch since passing it to Jarrod to help him heal after the rooftop. Her fingertips weren't tingling, no itching burn pressing her to pass. She flashed back to the night of the rave, when she'd spread too much Touch and it'd made her sick. Maybe that had been the cause of her stomach pains last night.

The train squealed into the station. The urge to get off, to turn around and go home, almost overwhelmed her. Az's arm came around her. His chin fell to the top of her head.

"I don't know how we're going to tell Kristen. She's gonna blame me," Eden said. She turned into Az's shoulder so he wouldn't see the hurt and guilt.

If she'd done better on the roof and gotten Az out of there before Gabe had shown up, things would have ended differently. Gabe's sin, the one that had caused his Fall, had been taking a life. Hers.

Gabe had known Eden would turn into a Sider after her death. He'd sped up the process to keep her safe from Luke, and it had cost him everything.

"Gabe made his choices," Az said. "He knew it was a mortal sin. He did it anyway." He kept his gaze on the list of subway stops above them, the next one lit with a red light. "I think Kristen's going to be more worried about finding him than blaming you."

Eden had the distinct feeling Kristen wouldn't be so civil once she knew she'd lost her best friend because of Eden. "Gabriel would want her to know, right? He'd want her to know he didn't just leave?"

"Honestly? Gabe's dangerous. I think we're putting her in more danger telling her what happened." Az wouldn't look at her as the train's brakes squealed. "I don't know if we should be looking for him at all."

She stared at him as the doors opened. It was their stop. She got up and didn't look back.

They surfaced onto street level, and Eden's phone vibrated in her pocket. The icon for a voice mail flashed on her screen. She slowed so Az could catch up as she dialed in to check it.

His head was down, his movements slow and methodical. Eden dropped back to him, a pang of worry stirring in her stomach. "You all right?" she asked.

He seemed to catch himself, snapping a smile on as he lifted his head. She held up a finger, her attention on the voice mail. She hadn't recognized the number, but she sure as hell recognized the voice.

"It's *Madeline*," Eden said. Even the name set her on edge. No one had ever been specific about why Madeline was so terrible. Maybe it'd all been blown out of proportion, but Eden wasn't naïve enough to think there wasn't a kernel of truth in there somewhere.

"Eden, hey! It's Maddy! I hope you don't mind me calling, but we have a common adorable who seems to have been sullied with a bit of a scandal!" Eden could practically hear the sweetness oozing from her. *A common adorable?* she thought. "At this point, I figured it'd be in our best interests to team up and help Gabriel out. A little birdy told me you hopped a train bound for the Bronx, so I'm guessing you're headed to Kristen's. Maybe you could give me a call before you see her? I need to talk to you. It won't take long."

"What?" Az asked. When she didn't answer, he stopped her in the middle of the sidewalk. "Eden, what'd she say?"

Eden managed to snap the phone shut. "She knows we're here. She knows we're going to Kristen's." She glanced up. "Az, she mentioned Gabe. Something about a scandal." It screamed of a trap, but it was far too obvious to actually *be* a trap. "She wants me to call her before we go to Kristen's."

She wrapped her arms around herself, the phone still clutched in her hand.

Az pressed his lips together, staring up at the sky. She almost missed his soft curse, but his tension was undeniable. Even with the thick parka he wore, she could see the stiffness in his stance.

Once Kristen knew what happened to Gabe, Eden would lose her alliance. Her best bet was to hear Madeline

out. She flipped the phone open, hit Send, and put it to
her ear.

"Wait, before you call her I—"

"Eden!" Madeline said cheerily after barely one ring.
Az's shoulders slumped as the call connected. "My God,
how are you? These last few weeks have been insane!"
Eden thought she heard her stifle a giggle. "Really, you
and I should have gotten together ages ago, but, well, you
seemed kind of Team Kristen." Something in her voice
shifted, hardened a bit, though the light cadence stayed
the same. "How's that working out for you?"

"Fine." Her voice broke. She swallowed. "You mentioned Gabe," she said. "That's what I'm interested in."

"Meet me," Madeline said urgently. "You just got off
the train, right?"

"Yes."

"Look up. A block or so in front of you there's a blue
sign sticking off the front of the building. Says 'laundry'
in big white letters."

Eden glanced ahead. "I see it."

"I was told you're not alone. Is Az with you?" The
wind picked up, snowflakes swirling in thin lines across
the sidewalk. Eden wondered how long Madeline's "little
birdy" had been following them. Maybe they'd only been
seen getting on the train. It would have been fairly obvious where they were going. At least enough to make an

educated guess. Still, Madeline had had them tailed and neither had noticed.

"Yes, he's with me," Eden answered, unnerved.

"Even better."

I bet, she thought. "We'll be there in a few." She didn't wait for an answer before she hung up and pointed ahead.

"Laundry," she said to Az. She grabbed his hand as they started walking again. With every step they took closer to the Laundromat, the snowflakes seemed to multiply. "I don't like this. Adam says . . ." She paused, faltering. "He used to say . . ." For a split second, a perfect memory of Adam played through her mind, the first morning at Kristen's when he'd stolen her bacon from her breakfast platter. She could almost hear his laugh. Before he'd told her how he'd felt about her, before Az had come back and she'd turned Adam down. Before Adam's betrayal had led them all to the roof and Libby had turned him to ash. Sent him Downstairs.

"Eden?" Az's careful tone snapped her back to reality.

"Yeah, I just . . . Sorry." She cleared her throat. Eden couldn't be sure she'd spoken Adam's name aloud since everything had happened. She was prepared to feel hate, but not the hurt ache filling her chest. "Adam said once that Kristen wasn't the worst. Madeline scared the shit out of him. She knew we were on the train, that you were with me. She's having us followed, Az. I should call Jarrod and warn him in case she's got someone on him, too."

Az let out a long breath, shifting ahead of her. "Look, Eden, there's something you should know about Madeline. I should have told you before, but Gabe didn't want anyone to know."

They were still two shops down, but the door to the Laundromat swung open, Madeline's head popping around the door.

He leaned closer under the guise of a kiss he planted near Eden's ear, his whisper urgent. "Madeline knows about Gabe. Don't answer any of her questions if you can help it, understand?"

Surprise kept her frozen, but couldn't help the sting of his words. "You kept that from me?"

Az lifted his head to Madeline and didn't answer. She bounded toward them in something between a skip and a run.

"Look, she's already doing her straight-to-business face!" Madeline's smile seemed fastened to her lips, fake enough that it could pass for a prop, glued over her real mouth. Her attention shifted to Az, her tone playful. "You make scorching arm candy for someone who was supposed to be dead."

"Yeah," he said. "Turns out the afterlife is boring no matter how you get there."

Madeline snickered. "I'm glad you decided to stick

around." Her tone darkened. "How are you doing?" Eden remembered Madeline's face at Kristen's ball, how she'd paled and panicked when Eden had told her about Az's "accident."

How well does he know her? Eden wondered. *And why the hell didn't I hear about it?*

Madeline glanced over at Eden. "Wow. Now *that* is a death glare."

From the corner of her eye, Eden caught Az scoping the street around them. They'd stepped off to the side, but were mostly out in the open. Whether on purpose or not, Madeline had made them easy targets.

Eden fought to keep the fear from her face. If Madeline knew about Gabe, that meant she really did have her rumored connections to the Fallen. No one else knew what had happened on that roof but Lucifer.

"You're used to dealing with Kristen," Madeline said, her eyes sharpening to a glittery emerald green. She crossed her arms, her neck drowned in the enormous fluffy scarf wrapped around it. "Ten thousand games that lead to one tiny nugget of a useless fact. She drives me crazy, Eden. Can we skip the drama?"

"I think that'd be best. You mentioned Gabriel." Eden kept her tone even, neither challenging nor inquisitive, simply stating a fact. She didn't react when Az took her hand, unsure whether it mattered if they appeared as a united front, if Madeline was a threat at all. *He promised me no more secrets,* she thought bitterly, and once again she was at a disadvantage because he'd kept something from her.

"I know that you spent a lovely sunrise on top of a building a few weeks ago." Madeline pointed to Az. "You were there, and you were there."

"What is this, *The Wizard of Oz?*" Eden forced the sarcasm.

"What do you want, Madeline?" Az asked. A sharp twinge in Eden's stomach made her breath catch. She pressed her lips together to hide her distress, but luckily Az's attention was on Madeline.

"God, you are completely set on ruining my good mood, aren't you?" A bitter cold breeze swept past them, whipping a chunk of Madeline's bangs loose from her bun. She unsnapped her barrette and yanked the red strands back where they belonged.

"I'm guessing it wasn't a breakfast get-together. And I wasn't invited." Madeline's gaze lingered on Eden before it shifted to Az. "You're being awful picky about who you trust these days. Have you told Eden all the secrets yet?"

Az squeezed Eden's shoulder. Her pain grew worse, stabbing.

She ripped away and spun on him, her breaths sharp. "Told me what secrets?" she demanded.

"On account of her love of causing strife, most of the Siders think Madeline sticks with the Fallen. In truth, she plays spy for both the Fallen *and* me and Gabe." His tone wasn't friendly. "Though I'm pretty sure Luke would be pissed to find that out."

Madeline chuckled. "I'd say that's accurate. Speaking of, Luke was on cloud nine, pardon the out-of-place Upstairs reference. Now, though, not so much. When I asked him what was up, he mumbled something about complications with Gabe."

Seconds ticked away, the traffic sloshing by. A thin layer of snow had accumulated, already turning to slush on the road. "You shouldn't have done things this way, Madeline." Az toed at the concrete. "I can't talk about Gabe with you. Not now."

Under Eden's ribs, pressure grew. Her entire abdomen and chest cavity clenched. She grabbed reflexively for Az's hand, squeezing it harder than she intended. A whimper escaped her, but then she felt a soft pop, and the pain vanished instantly. The relief brought tears to her eyes as she slowly exhaled. It was so much worse than the aching she'd felt after taking in too much Touch.

"According to what Luke's told me, being newly Fallen, Gabe should be on some sort of bloody rampage," Madeline went on, oblivious. "He's not. I mean, last time I saw—"

"Stop." A shudder passed through Az. His fists curled and uncurled at his sides, tension rolling off him in waves. Eden couldn't catch a look at his eyes, but she bet they'd changed from their normal blue.

"Az?" Eden said.

"Anything else." His voice cracked. He allowed only Eden a flash of his eyes, the dark navy spreading like smoke past his irises and into the whites. "Talk about anything else but him."

She jumped when Az dropped to one knee, reaching for him before she managed to stand up straight again. "Madeline, how are things in Queens?" Eden choked out.

Madeline's eyes flicked down to where Az knelt, his shoulders rising and falling with his deep breaths. "There was," Madeline said carefully, "another reason I wanted to talk to you. That's why I really called you."

Eden tore her attention away from Az, waiting.

"You can kill Siders," Madeline said bluntly.

Eden hesitated for only a fraction of a second. "Yes."

Madeline bounced on her toes. "I'm not sure if Kristen told you, but there's been a bit of . . . restructuring in the other boroughs. It didn't go well. So, I was wondering if there was a chance you'd work on commission."

Eden cocked her head. "What, like a hit? You want me to take someone out for you?" She scoffed. "I don't think so."

"Hear me out," Madeline said, moving a gloved hand to Eden's arm when she turned back to Az. "You've been hanging out in Manhattan, but it's not your territory. It's Erin's."

"It *was* Erin's." Eden stiffened. The day she'd left Kristen's house, Kristen had told her Erin was gone— made it seem like she'd done something to her to get her out. Eden hadn't questioned it. For some reason she'd assumed the girl was dead, even though it wasn't possible. "You're doing this now?" Eden said in disbelief, her eyes flashing to Az.

"Relax." Madeline forced a smile. "Eden, you've got a skewed picture of things, I promise. Kristen treats the rest of us like enemies, pretends she needs to hold on to her little stronghold like we're going to yank it out from under her. Really we thought it'd be best to spread out so we can find the new Siders. We didn't want them to be alone for longer than they have to be. It was difficult for us, when we didn't have each other. And we didn't want the Bound to notice us." Her brow furrowed for a brief moment. "The rest of us couldn't care less about territories and her silly alliances. She's our friend, but her paranoid quirks really are paranoid quirks."

Eden's eyebrow rose. "A second ago you asked me to kill one of you. Yeah, she's totally paranoid. Sure."

"Honestly, it's an isolated incident, I promise," Madeline said, her tone soft but confident. "Vaughn's selling Touch to the mortals. Like a drug. He had a whole crew of Siders in on the operation. As soon as the rest of us found out, Erin went to Staten Island. We asked him to stop; he didn't. We used force, but it didn't seem to faze him. Honestly, at this point I don't care what happens to him. He's putting us all in danger by being so blatant. Especially now that the Bound know about us."

Eden bristled. She feigned disinterest, dropping down next to Az. The safest bet was to get them both out of there and grill Az on what Madeline knew later. "We'll go as soon as you're ready," she whispered, and stood. "Look, Madeline. That's not my thing."

"I'll make it worth your while."

She couldn't consider the offer, not now that anyone she killed only increased Luke's numbers, but Madeline thinking of her as a last option gave her a bit of power. "What're you offering?"

"What's valuable to you? We need to make this happen."

Something about Madeline's words hit her. She couldn't give her false hope. If she wasn't going to be able to take out the Siders anymore, what did it matter if everyone knew? They'd find out eventually. Better from her. Eden opened her mouth.

Az grabbed her leg, startling her. "We need to go. I need . . ." He squeezed his eyes shut tighter and bit his lip. "Now." He stood and leaned into Eden, speaking low enough that only she would hear. "It's not getting better."

Her heart thumped hard in her chest. "Okay, we've got this," she said, with a calm she wasn't even close to feeling. She couldn't keep the desperation from her face when she turned to the other girl. "Madeline, we have to grab a cab."

Madeline headed to the corner, her arm raised. Eden helped Az to the curb as the cab pulled up.

"Thank you," she said to Madeline, slipping into the car beside Az. She gave the driver the address distractedly, her attention on Az as the car drove off, leaving Madeline behind.

Eden rested her head on his shoulder, her lips against his ear. She forgot about Madeline's offer, the cab, the world. "I'm with you," she said to him, soft as a lullaby. "I'll always be with you, right here next to you. I love you."

She ran her fingers up the side of his neck, gently tilted him closer. He dropped against her shoulder, and she moved a subtle hand to his back. Under her fingers, his wings trembled.

"I am *not* leaving you," he grated out, his arm wrapping around her. The tightness of it stole her breath. His chest heaved, and under her hand his wings flexed, straining against the ace bandage she knew would be wrapped tight to keep them hidden.

"Fight it," she whispered. "You fight it. Don't you dare leave me."

His lips rose from her shoulder to her neck. He kissed her there, his hands winding into her hair. Desire ripped through her at the intensity, his skin hot against hers. He pulled back suddenly, drawing a breath.

"Shhh," she murmured.

"They can't make me go." Every word came softer, trepidation in each one, as if he didn't quite believe what he said.

"I know," she said, running her hand through his hair. A tiny knot of dread tightened inside her heart.

Only talking about Gabe had set him off this time.

He was getting worse, getting weaker.

Az lowered his head back onto the seat, his breathing slow and even, his eyes closed, though she knew he couldn't be sleeping. He looked younger when the tension left his face.

She pulled her phone from her pocket, careful not to jostle Az. If Luke was angry, maybe Gabe wasn't as evil as he'd hoped. Maybe . . . Maybe he was still himself enough that he would help Az. She hesitated and then typed out a text to the last number that had called her.

He needs Gabe back. You need Vaughn dead. Find me Gabriel first, and then I'll handle Vaughn.

* * *

Eden lowered her head to the back of the seat, watching Az silently. Taking out Vaughn meant she would be sending him Downstairs. The thought made her sick. On the seat beside her, Az heaved a sigh. She ran a finger down his temple, across his cheek and chin, knowing she'd made her decision.

"Whatever it takes," she whispered.

CHAPTER 5

Kristen's hands were freezing, curled into fists and tucked against the folds of her dress. *How did I get here?* she thought, panicked, suddenly aware of the bench she sat on, the empty park around her. She shook her head, tossing free the snow that had settled on her hair, and wrapped her bare arms around herself. Her teeth had stopped chattering. How long ago, she wasn't sure.

Think. There has to be an explanation.

You knew this would happen, her mind argued. *You're slipping without Gabe.*

Her jaw felt wired shut. For a split second, she felt the wires, hardware glued to her teeth holding her mouth shut. *Not real. It's not real.* The feeling faded. She took in a huge stuttered gasp of air. She'd banished the hallucination. It was all the proof she needed. "I am *not* slipping."

Not yet.

The Bound. The thought came from nowhere.

"My God," she whispered. Gabe had been able to read her thoughts. Maybe others who were Bound would be able to put thoughts *there*. "That's it. It has to be."

Her breath clouded, hovering before it dissipated. Would Gabe have been angry enough to tell the Bound about the Siders? She shook her head. No, if he did, they would come after his precious Eden, too.

Gabriel had worked so hard to hide the Siders away, keep them a secret so the Bound wouldn't have them destroyed. But maybe they hadn't needed Gabe. Maybe they'd found her anyway. Discovered the Siders. Were tormenting her.

"Get out of my head," she commanded. "I know what you're doing. You're trying to make me think I'm going crazy, but I'm not!"

She heard a stick snap behind her. Footsteps crunching in the snow. "Kristen?"

"No. You leave me alone." Her voice broke. Gabriel had told her how the Bound did what they felt needed to be done. Miracles took second seat to plagues, death, and destruction. They would torture her. Use her to find out how to kill the other Siders.

If there was anyone there at all.

She squeezed her eyes shut. "I'm not playing your games. I know you're not there."

Pressure on her shoulder. A hand.

So real.

"Kristen, open your eyes." The footsteps rounded the corner of the bench. The rustle of fabric as someone—*no, you're imagining this*—as she imagined someone squatting down.

"No one's there." She leaned forward, rocking against her knees. A touch of fingertips, a hand pushing her back, forcing her to straighten. She shuddered. It felt so real.

"Open your eyes," the voice demanded.

"I'm not going crazy," she whispered.

"Going? From the look of you that line got crossed some time ago, my romantic hopeless."

She didn't bother answering. Sane people didn't answer voices.

"Kristen?" Tender tones now. New tactics. *Beware,* some part of her mind cried. *They'll trick you.* When he spoke again, any semblance of kindness had disappeared from his voice. "You're in the park. You're also covered in snow, and it's freezing out. Now, clearly you weren't *batshit* when you called me—"

"I did not call anyone." She pressed her lips together.

"It's Luke, Kristen." Her breath caught. Slowly, she opened her eyes.

He was only inches from her face, flakes of snow caught in his black curls. He reached out to her, and in her shock, her hand left her lap, found his. A smile flashed across his lips at the contact, satisfaction glinting in the obsidian of his eyes.

"You called," he said. "And I came to you." He rose off his knees in one lithe move and slid beside her on the bench.

"I . . ." she trailed off. "No. No, you stay away from me." She squeezed his hand for a second, long enough to feel the bones, make sure it was real before she tossed it away. "You don't get to talk to me ever again."

"Today hasn't been so good?" He said it like she'd missed her bus or misplaced her keys. She hesitated, but his smile broke her down. There was no pity in it. He took her hands again, rubbing his over them slowly to generate warmth.

She glanced around. Everything lay under at least an inch of fresh snow. The lamps along the path were lit, fooled by the cloud cover, though it wasn't yet dark. She blinked as the wind shifted into her face. Save for herself and Luke, the park was empty. No one would see her talking to him.

Her fingers felt frozen, mottled with patches of maroon and white. Luke followed her gaze down to their hands.

"Could you go, please?" She heard the desperate plea in it, knew before he answered that it wouldn't be that easy.

"Come on, you know I'm not going to leave you."

She licked her lips, and they seemed to freeze almost instantly.

Anxiety flooded through her. How long had she been gone? Had anyone else seen her leave? Why couldn't she have called Sebastian? Her face crumpled, and Luke lowered his voice. "No one has to know you let me help. It can be our secret."

"I don't want anything from you," she whispered. His name already sullied too many of her secrets.

"None of this is your fault. You shouldn't have to go through this." She searched his eyes, waiting for some sign that he played her, malice hidden in the darkest corners, but found none.

"Kristen," he said, slouching forward to rest his elbows on his knees. His fingers rubbed the bridge of his nose, ran across his high cheekbone to tuck his hair behind his ear. He scooted closer. "Let me inside."

She heard a faint pop, the sound of static. Even her own diseased brain reacted in fear. She'd only let him do it once. Too easily she remembered the slippery shivers, the dangerous thrill of opening her mind to him. Fallen or not, he had the same skills as Gabe when it came to fixing her brain. "No." Panic rose in her throat. "I shouldn't have come here."

"Kristen, stop." He gripped her chin, forced her to face him. She kept her eyes closed, her lips pressed tight.

A giggle broke out. Kristen whimpered as she realized it came from neither of them. It grew into a laugh, echoing around in her head. *What will he do when she loses her mind in his clutches?* a small voice asked.

A ricocheting cacophony burst through her skull. *She would never Are you sure She wouldn't dare But he has the same talents as This one crossed her, betrayed her, and she won't make that mistake again Never let him in*

Never let him in.

"I'm asking your permission." Luke's voice. Louder than the others. "Kristen, you can't make me see you like this," he snarled, and then his voice softened as he took her hands. "Open your eyes. Let me help you. No catch."

Her breath came in short gasps. Soon she'd be drowning in the madness. She'd never be able to hold out for Gabe.

Luke's lying He cares nothing for her It's all a game If she gives in he wins

"Shut up!" she screamed. She wanted to yank her hands over her ears, but Luke had her hands.

Just this once. Letting him in even a little would give her time to reach Gabe—hell, she'd go through Az if she had to—and apologize a thousand times. She swallowed hard, her heart slamming in her chest. She only needed a little help, would let Luke in for a few seconds, no more.

What if it's a trick? She cleared her mind as best she

could. Banished thoughts of Gabe, Eden, Az. And then she opened her eyes.

"Do it quickly," she choked out.

His fingers wound gently around the back of her head, massaging into her hair, but she was barely aware, locked into the black pupils, the absence of light concentrated in the center of his eyes.

She felt the connection take, the cool sizzle of him sliding into her skull. His breath hit her lips. The static dialed up, a scream of white noise, then again, louder. *Get him out.*

She managed to lift her arms, pushing him away as her clarity came back. "Stop," she murmured. "Stop."

Luke untangled from her hair when she started to resist, squeezed her shoulders. "I need to finish."

"STOP!" she screamed.

He turned his head, and the noise snapped off. Everything dulled. Kristen blinked hard, sudden tears of relief and embarrassment caught in her lashes. Luke. She'd let Luke into her head. Again. Shame rolled over her.

"I wasn't done!"

She jerked her shoulders out of his grasp, staggering to her feet. "Stay away from me."

"Kristen!" he called after her, louder as she made her way out of the park. "It won't last!"

Luke stayed where she'd left him on the bench. She

quickened her steps anyway. Not to see if he'd chase, only to get her blood pumping again, to get warm. Nothing more.

She pushed the thought of him from her mind, her scalp still tingling where his fingers had pressed tight.

CHAPTER 6

For half an hour, the demons had been trailing Gabe from subway car to subway car. They were there with him as he switched trains. He couldn't shake them. They didn't look mortal, not to him, their faces slowly melting downward, starting over at their foreheads like eternity pools. The humans passed by them, not one of them reacting. The demons were beyond the capabilities of human eyes. He would have thought, being Fallen, that the minions of Hell would be on his side.

He was wrong. Perhaps it was because he resisted the dark urges.

A sharp pain shot through his upper arm. Gabe didn't look back, quickened his pace.

The demons stood behind him as he waited on the platform, growing more brazen with every passing minute. He gritted his teeth, shifted his arm away, rubbing it through his coat. Fingers closed over his, clammy reptilian skin, brushing away his own hand. The same pinch on the back of his arm came again. This time he couldn't stifle his cry. Behind him, the demons cackled in glee.

"His suffers taste like sugar!" The demon girl's voice crackled like glass through the freezing air. "Sweet sorrows," she said, and Gabe heard the mocking pout in it.

"Touch me again and I'll have your hands," he said without turning around. Pain shot up the back of his arm. He turned, his lips curling up, and hissed at them. They found this hysterical, practically falling all over themselves as they followed him through the station. Gabe glanced around at the mortals on the platform, but not one met his eyes. To them, he was only a ranting lunatic. It was only then that he saw the penknife in the demon boy's hand, the thin blade bloodied. He wondered what the mortals would think when the blood soaked through his jacket.

"Bound and broken, sins are spoken. Doesn't make you one of us," the demon boy said in singsong. He reached forward again and Gabe grabbed the hand, squeezing until he heard bones crack. The knife clattered to the ground, but the girl demon was on it before Gabe had a chance to dive for it. When Gabe released the boy, the demon shook out his hand. The broken bones rattled down into the skin of his fingers, filling them like balloons stuffed with rocks.

The demon girl's fingers shot forward, her nails gouging out a chunk of Gabe's exposed skin near his wrist.

"You're dark as daylight, Failed One. We'll have you piece by piece."

Gabe pressed forward, away from them. In front of him, a mortal boy stumbled in the yellow-painted caution area before the sunken tracks. He caught his footing, moved back from the edge, and shot Gabe a glare. Around him the crowd had grown uncomfortably silent. He could sense their fear of him, the way they leaned away like a receding tide. The platform was too crowded for them to move far.

"I'm sorry," Gabe mumbled, trying to give the teenager room.

The girl demon cackled in his ear. "Apologizing to mortals when he should be slaughtering them?" The sharp laugh dropped to a guttural snarl. "You want the scent of his blood on your skin. The thought pleases you, does it not?"

The crowd on the platform strained forward toward the tracks, restless.

"Newly Fallen. No resisting the urge," one demon laughed to the other. "The boy's brains will butter our bread."

Gabe focused on the back of the boy's jacket. He hated himself for the quaking in his arms, the muscles jerking as he fought not to raise them. He hated how much effort it took to not give in, his quickened breaths, spiking adrenaline. *Push him, fetch agonies.* The hot need overwhelmed everything. Newspapers stirred, swirling on currents. A train approached. So little to tip him forward.

A whimper rose from Gabe's throat, but he cut it short. The demons curled closer, sensing his weakness, oozing around him as if their bodies were part smoke. With every dark cell of his body, he willed the train to come. Push the boy in front of it.

"No!" Gabe clenched his hands at his sides.

Fetid breath skated across his cheek. "Why ache for slaughter? Don't deny yourself!"

What harm to kill only one?

"How glorious to bathe in his blood."

Gabe barely registered the press of the penknife into his palm. His fingers curled around it unconsciously.

"Slit him open. Ear to ear."

Breakable, so breakable. Mortals crawled through these tunnels like rats. A plague of decaying flesh, rotting cell by cell, day by day. His foot slid forward of its own volition. His gaze rose to the pale skin of the boy's throat.

"No." Gabe tore his eyes away, staring down the hollow tunnel.

"Wicked wants. They're inside you. You can't forsake the darkness." A breath of words across his ear. "Kill him."

"Kill him," the other cooed.

Gabe trembled. No, the platform beneath him trembled. He sighed in relief. Thirty seconds and the train would be there. Twenty. Ten.

The knife was jerked out of Gabe's hand. He yelled as it stabbed into his own shoulder, biting deep. He yanked away from the blinding pain and slammed into the mortal. The train clattered; brakes screamed.

Everything happened too fast to stop. The boy stumbled forward, sneaker laces caught under Gabe's boot. The horn blaring. A wet smack. Fluid sprayed across Gabe's face.

Only the boy's arm remained. It stood up straight, crushed in the gap between the platform and the now-stopped train. The fingers twitched, waving good-bye with the final death spasms.

Around him, chaos broke out. The crowd panicked as they realized what had happened. Screams echoed through the train station.

Gabe lunged up the stairs. It was an accident. He retched, dry heaving at the first trickle of regret. His body sought out the feeling, expelled it from him like a poison. A pair of police officers rushed down the stairs to the subway, walkie-talkies shouting codes.

Gripping the stair rail, Gabe hauled himself up to the street. The image of the arm with its waggling fingers burned behind his eyelids with each blink, stained upon his retina. Find another thought. Anything.

His brain sputtered through images of steaming intestines, rivulets of blood drying on concrete. He pushed past them, searching, his desperation growing as he grasped for anything that could calm him, soothe the need for fury and knuckles smearing against brick walls like cheese graters. Flayed flesh. Gabe fell to his knees.

He'd lose it, lose control. Rampage. "No, please," he cried.

Pedestrians marched around him. Soon they'd be begging for their lives. And he'd ignore their pleas. Kill slowly.

"No," he moaned as the ice began to fill him, drag him down into another cold night of foggy memories made of half-forgotten nightmares. "I won't give in. Not again."

And then he saw her face. Behind his closed eyes, Kristen's face shimmered like a mirage. Gabe sucked a breath, focused. Something too much like affection overwhelmed him, and his stomach rolled uneasily. Kristen. He fed off her quiet strength, felt the ice inside him ease back a bit. He heard her whisper his name, the old name.

You are not Gabriel anymore, he cursed himself. *You're a murderer. Dangerous. You killed Eden.*

"I'm sorry." His whisper faltered, broke apart in the freezing air. The darkness smelled of snow to come.

"I won't kill again," he spat, rising to his feet. And it was true. He'd gotten stronger.

A little longer. A bit more control. One day without a blackout—only one—and he'd trust himself enough to track down Az. Az could help him. Help him get Home.

"I belong Upstairs." Gabe lurched as the word left his lips, hitting the concrete on his hands and knees. He puked until his stomach burned, the bile stained with strings of red.

"I want to go Home," he choked out defiantly.

The retching started anew.

CHAPTER 7

$\mathcal{E}$den braced herself against the sink, her knuckles white. She caught her reflection in the mirror, tears smearing black streaks of mascara down her cheeks. She'd have to redo her makeup.

"Are you coming or not?" Az yelled from the living room. "We gotta get going."

She sucked a breath, tried to keep her voice from wavering as she yelled, "I need a minute!"

Pain racked through her. As it had earlier that morning, the pressure in her guts built. This time was so much worse. She doubled over with a moan. A strange gurgle rose out of her as the cramp finally broke off. Her mouth filled with a horrid taste.

She slammed on the faucet, cupping a handful of water and swishing it around in her cheeks. When she spat, the water came out gray.

Eden stared as it swirled down the drain. She startled at the rap on the bathroom door.

"You get lost?" Az asked. Even through the wood, she could hear his boyish excitement.

The change in him was unsettling. Mere hours ago, he'd been dangerously close to Falling, but with every mile they put between themselves and Madeline, he'd rallied. By the time they'd reached the apartment, he'd been his own self. She wondered what he'd stopped Madeline from saying, what other drama their hasty exit had spared him. He'd recovered so quickly, almost as if he hadn't really been Falling. She shook away the thought.

"I'm coming!" she called back, and then lowered her voice to a whisper, staring back at her reflection in the mirror. "You've gotta tell him about this," she said quietly to herself. She stifled a gag and cupped another drink. This time the water left her mouth clear.

Even before her mystery pain, she'd tried to back out of their date, reason with him, but he wouldn't budge. She gave in when she realized how much their night together meant to him. Az needed this. But it didn't keep her fears away. She knew he wanted to make the night special, a surprise, but that only raised her anxiety. Would they be in a crowd? Alone? What if something happened and Az lost it again? She glanced down at the swirl of residue left around the drain.

What if something happened to her?

Eden wet the washcloth hanging over the back of the faucet and used a bit of soap to clean under her eyes, doing her best to be gentle.

She quickly stroked on a fresh layer of mascara. "Tonight's going to be good," she said, her voice shaking worse than her hands. "And tomorrow . . ."

You stop pretending this is going to go away, she thought. But for now, she plastered a smile on her lips. With a deep breath, Eden turned from the mirror and swung the door open, raising a hand to the doorframe.

"I swear on all that is holy, you laugh and it's your ass," she said, knowing Az would hear the nerves behind her bravado and hoping he'd think it was only her being girly about her hair.

Her bangs swept across her forehead, clipped back near her ear, but the rest of her hair she'd chopped off to nearly a pixie cut. The pink had been bleached away, and then she'd dyed the highlights a dark green.

The silence stretched out. As stupid as it was, she realized she really did want him to like what she'd done. At least not *hate* it. "I figured if anyone was looking for us, they'd be saying I had pink hair." Eden smiled uncomfortably. "Now I don't."

The rumors circulating about her since she'd moved to Manhattan always mentioned her pink streaks. That's how the Siders found her. If the Bound were doing the same, maybe the dye would throw them off. Even Luke wouldn't recognize her from the back, especially in a crowd. It might be enough to buy them one good night together.

Az rose off the couch slowly.

"Bad idea?" Eden brought her hand up to the back of her neck, catching a few strands of her newly cut hair. He swallowed hard and shook his head. "What, then?" she asked, hoping he hadn't heard her in the bathroom.

"Hair's fine, but in that dress, *everyone's* going to be looking at you."

"Nice, Az." She snorted, dropping her pose in the threshold, stooping to pull a strap of her high heel around her ankle and buckling it. Her dress was black, the white frill of the underlayer showing through tiny lacey eyelets. It was one of her favorite thrift store finds, but more importantly it went with her most comfortable heels. Ones she'd be able to run in.

Everything inside her told her it was a stupid risk, going out like this so they could pretend they were a normal couple. But as she watched Az grab his suit coat off the back of the couch and slip into it, the danger didn't seem so terrible. They'd be in public. They'd be together. She felt okay again.

Eden watched as he buttoned the blazer closed, mesmerized. She'd never seen him dressed up, hadn't prepared herself for the way the suit made him look—sophisticated and fashionable. The sharp lines of his jaw and cheekbones belonged in the pages of a magazine. On a movie screen. He looked up suddenly, caught her ogling him. His grin widened as he walked to her. And that smile, Az happy, made all the risk worth it.

"You know," she said, cocking her head. "I think we need to work more formal events into our schedule."

He smiled, adjusting his cuff links. "Yeah? You like me in a suit?"

She laced her hands around his neck. "Actually, right now I'm a little caught up on the idea of getting you *out* of the suit."

He kissed the line of her jaw, slowly working his way lower on her neck. A soft sigh slipped out of her. He smelled so good, his normal crisp scent mixing with the musk of the cologne he wore. Her fingers tensed on his shoulders.

"You're not trying to blow off our date again, are you," he whispered in her ear. She groaned, pulling back. Az caught her hand, lifted it until she moved closer again.

"No, but for the record"—she slid her leg slowly between his, her voice low and sultry—"I'm taking a rain check." She kissed his cheek, forcing herself to stop there, though every part of her wanted to keep going.

"For the record, you keep that up you're not going to need one," he murmured back.

She retreated to her room and grabbed the waist-length black coat she'd left on her bed, the silver gloves she knew she'd need in public. Out of Az's sight, she gave herself a moment. Nothing hurt, the strange taste washed away. *I'm fine,* she promised herself. *Everything's fine.*

"Ready?" she asked.

Az nodded as he hooked her arm, leading the way out the door and into the hall. He locked up behind them.

"So can we take the subway to our mystery location? We're already cutting it close on rent," she said as they walked down the stairs.

"Love on the cheap means I'm going to have to amp up the romance." He threw the downstairs door open with a dramatic sweeping gesture, catching the tips of her fingers as if she were a princess climbing from a coach. "Your stairs await, m'lady."

She laughed and stepped through. Someone let out a sharp exhale and the stairs came alive with motion, legs and arms tangling in the frantic rush to stand, a small chorus of pleas. Eden froze as the three Siders formed a semicircle around her.

"Don't even ask her!" Az was in front of her before she could react. "She's out of commission."

A tremor passed through Eden, phantom pains shooting up her arms, across her collarbones. A month ago she would have already been leading the three to the alley, ending them one by one and taking their Touch into herself. Saving them from an existence they couldn't escape. But that was before. Now, death at her lips would send a soul Downstairs. To Luke. She hadn't taken out a Sider since Gabe had Fallen.

The pains in her arms sharpened. *It's happening again,* she thought, trying not to panic, but the sensation faded.

"We're not leaving." One guy came forward, his hand held out. In it was a fifty-dollar bill, the price she'd charged for her "talents." "I have the money. She has to do it."

"No. She doesn't." Az's voice rang with authority. "Spread the word. We'll let you know when things change."

"I'm sorry." Eden couldn't keep the guilt from her voice. The ones who sought her out were desperate, but she wouldn't send them Downstairs. Without her, no one was going anywhere. They'd have to learn to make the best of it.

The guy reached in his pocket, digging frantically. "Look, take it all. I mean, I won't need it, right?" Eden peeked over Az's shoulder. The Sider's eyes found hers. "Please?"

"I can't," she managed, taking Az's hand and pushing past.

"Bitch!" one of them yelled out behind her.

Az stiffened, but Eden kept walking. "They can call me

whatever they want. It doesn't matter." She forced herself to smile. "And we're not letting it ruin tonight."

They headed down the stairs to the subway station, swiping their MetroCards as they passed through the turnstiles. Eden was a step ahead, made it a few yards before she realized Az wasn't following. Behind her, he walked slowly, looking intently at his hand. She watched as he lifted it to his nose and sniffed uncertainly.

"Get something on you?"

He glanced up and held out his hand. On his palm was a smear of black. "I think there was something on the turnstile. Was it on yours, too?"

She turned her hand over. The entire center of her palm was covered in gray-black powder.

"The turnstile," she said absently, brushing her hands together. She scraped her nails against the powder. It flaked away, the skin underneath clean.

Az shrugged, wiping his palms on the legs of his trouser pants, and started walking toward the train again.

"Want to try to guess where we're going yet?" Az asked.

"No idea." Eden forced a smile, trying to let herself get caught up in his excitement.

Az grinned coyly, listing off on his fingers. "Someplace very public, where if anyone did see us, they wouldn't dare make a scene. Free. Cheesy romantic." He paused. "It's December," he prodded.

She gave an amused shrug as they boarded the train.

His smile widened. "Then you'll have to wait."

She'd never seen anything so beautiful. The evergreen rose high above them, every branch twinkling with lights.

Az stood behind her, snuggling close. "It's your first Christmas in the city," he said. "I wanted to be the one to show you the tree."

Eden laughed, giddy as she took in the nearly hundred-foot-tall Rockefeller Center tree. "I *think* you might have outdone yourself on the romance factor."

She turned into his arms, hugging him. Beside them, a busker played Christmas carols on a tattered violin, the soulful notes echoing through the still air. Eden dropped a dollar into the musician's case as they passed.

Az's hand caught her waist suddenly, twirling her with the momentum. "Dance with me?" He smiled. "It'll keep me out of trouble."

His hands flexed, pulling her closer to him, and everything else seemed to melt away. He spun her, whirled her out until the tips of their gloved fingers were the only thing connecting them. Then his fingers called her closer, leading her back to him. Something shifted in his eyes. At first she thought it was only a subtle change in color, but there was more to it, a calm contentedness. *A perfect world*, she thought suddenly. *This is how we would be.* One of her hands held his, the other on his shoulder as they fell into step, a delicate back and forth.

Her breath caught as Az dropped her into a dip, swung her up again.

He adjusted his grip on Eden's waist, pulling her closer. "Told you everyone'd be watching you in that dress," he whispered. She glanced around, self-consciously realizing the crowd had parted in a circle of smiling faces. She tried to ignore the eyes on her, tried to concentrate on Az, but a blush heated her neck and she lost her step. He gripped her hand, spun her away from him. Her dress billowed. She tightened her arm until his had wrapped back around her.

The crowd clapped and folded in around them, going back to the normal strolling pedestrian traffic.

"You look gorgeous." Az kissed her forehead, her cheek, her earlobe. "It's going to be okay," he whispered, running his hands up and down her arms. "I know you're worried about me. But no matter what happens, you and I are going to come out of this okay and together, all right? Just like last time."

She nodded, her arms circling him. Everything in her wanted to kiss him, lips against his, breathing his breath. But she couldn't. Something in her breath could kill the other Siders. And her lips were poisonous to Az. She'd already passed him Touch once accidently, and he'd nearly

Fallen. They'd never be able to kiss. She tried not to think about it, to be satisfied with his lips on her neck. It was the penance to pay for being with him. One she'd suffer through every day if it meant staying together. "I'm glad you convinced me to come out."

"I wouldn't have let you miss—" Az stopped mid-sentence. Her head on his shoulder, Eden felt him tense. "Jesus Christ," he whispered, his voice betraying a fear she'd never heard in him before.

She didn't dare move. "What? What is it?"

"Go. Run."

Her hand slid down to his chest. "No. I'm not leaving you alone."

"Please!"

She opened her mouth to protest and felt his heart speed up. Az kept his eyes over her shoulder, her hand still gripped in his.

"Who is it? Luke?" She turned to scan the crowd behind her.

"It's not the Fallen," Az said in terrified disbelief.

The angel coming toward them looked almost human, but Eden picked him out of the crowd easily. He was too perfect to blend, his features too defined, his eyes all wrong, too fearless. His bowlegged gait carried him on a crooked path toward them, as if he had just learned to walk. He stayed silent until he was almost on top of them.

"You tarnished lag!" he snarled at Az. "Where is Gabriel?"

Eden jumped at the unchecked anger, her eyes widening. A few heads in the crowd turned their way and gave the three of them a once-over.

Az kept his voice calm, but the hand in hers trembled. "He's not here, Michael. I don't know where Gabe—"

"Call him proper!" Michael yelled. "Gab-ri-el." He split the name in three, voice cracking on the last syllable with a sound like twisting steel. Eden couldn't help her wince. "He's blackmarked and forbidden Upstairs. You have knowledge."

"You're forbidden from *leaving* Upstairs, or did you forget that little detail? Not unless it's the end times." Az lowered his voice to be sure they weren't being overheard; his eyes darted across the crowd. The violinist played on as if to mask their words, aided by the happy chatter of the mortals around them. "And that would be mortal end times, Michael. Losing your lover doesn't count."

Michael looked nauseated as Az spoke.

"See," Az went on, rotating slightly toward Eden, "Michael's the one who got me thrown out. For love. And now he's down here to save his own. Now *that* is irony."

Michael's trying to save his own love? Gabe couldn't be with *this guy,* she thought in shock.

"So covetous of revenge that you'd leave Gabriel

even Unfeathered? You *know* it shouldn't be so."

Az's face fell. "It wasn't my fault," he whispered. Eden wrapped her arm around his. *He's goading Az,* she thought, horrified. *The Bound wouldn't push him to Fall fully . . . would they?*

Michael's head swiveled suddenly to the side, birdlike, as he shuffled a few inches closer to Eden. She froze under his cold gray eyes. His nostrils flared, scenting her out like an animal. "She's one of those *things*, isn't she?"

That's it, she thought. *Pay attention to me.* It would keep him from messing with Az. Eden dropped Az's hand and stepped forward.

Michael stifled a gag with the back of his hand. "Her flesh reeks of smolder. How do you stand the stench?"

Eden balked. Az carefully annunciated each word he spoke. "She is *not* Damned."

"Nor are those the words I spoke. Shall I repeat? Her flesh . . . reeks . . . of smolder."

Even in the strange glow of the Christmas lights, Eden saw the color drain from Az's face. His worried eyes darted to her, skipped back to Michael. In the crowd, people were starting to watch them. Some had taken out their cell phones. If she could get Michael to react, someone would help. She and Az could make a run for it.

"Wow," Eden said with false enthusiasm. "Those are some stellar interpersonal skills you've got there, Mikey."

He snarled at the nickname, his teeth clacking as he snapped his jaw shut. "You know, Gabriel was my best friend. And yet he never mentioned the whole reeking thing. Go figure."

"His heart was kind. He's cursed now for the care he bestowed," Michael said with a sneer, glancing past her to Az. "Was it not enough to discard glories for soiled doves? Now you sully yourself with this *pestilence*?"

"I made my choice. If you want Eden, you're going to have to go through me."

"Not her," Michael said with a wicked lilt to his words. "It's you I come for, Azazel."

A shoulder bumped Eden. "We have a problem here?"

A gasp of relief burst from her as she caught the dark uniform out of the corner of her eye. Seriously, a cop when she actually wanted one around.

"No, sir. This asshole is leaving," Eden said quickly, and then shot him an apologetic smile for the swear and shrugged. "Boys!"

Michael did his weird head tilt again. The police officer raised an eyebrow, clearly not buying Eden's story, but unable to put together what was going on.

"I don't want to see you again, Michael. We're over!" Eden huffed. She grabbed Az's hand and stormed off into the crowd.

"Hey, wait!" she heard the cop yell after her, but knew

he wouldn't chase them. And if Michael tried, he'd be stopped. At least held up. Eden looked to Az beside her, caught the dark swirl of his eyes in the twinkle of lights from the tree.

"Faster," she said, darting them in the direction of the subway. She had to get him away from the crowd, from the danger of Michael—whoever Michael was—before he lost control.

CHAPTER 8

Jarrod yanked up his hood but the air whisked inside anyway, down the back of his neck.

Pulling the cords of his hoodie, he rebalanced the three coffee cups and worked his zipper with one hand as the door to Milton's closed behind him. He fumbled one of the cups, almost dropping it.

"Need some help?" someone asked. When he looked up, his smile faded. The girl who'd acted so strangely hours ago at the counter stood in front of him. She made a grab for one of the coffees nestled in the crook of his arm.

He recovered in time to twist out of her reach, even though he'd put his gloves on before heading outside. "Thanks, I'm good."

"I'm sorry, I just wanted to say hi," she said, following behind him down the sidewalk.

He paused before the crosswalk, and her shoulders rose in an apologetic shrug.

"I saw you inside?" she offered, as if the reason he was blowing her off had anything to do with not remembering her. She held out a hand. "I'm Sullivan."

"Sorry." Jarrod took a subtle step back. "My hands are full."

"Well, I offered to help. Still stands." The girl laughed when he shook his head. "I'm not freaking you out, am I? Honestly, I'm only trying to be friendly. Are you sure you don't want some help?" Her words sped up the more she talked, until they sounded almost frantic. Her hand floated there between them, waiting, begging to be touched. "Do you live near here?" she asked.

As her attempt at friendly banter failed, her body language changed. She seemed like she was coiled in on herself, ready to spring at him any second. Her eyes locked on him.

Jarrod backed away from her. He'd never seen a mortal with that look. It reminded him of the look the Siders on the stairs had, driven dangerous with desperation. Her insistence on trying to shake his hand was a little too deliberate, a challenge, like he'd fail some test if he didn't do it.

"I'm actually busy. See ya," he said, searching for a break in the traffic he could take advantage of instead of hoping for the crosswalk light to switch.

"Wait," she said. "Please." He turned back, raising an eyebrow. She shifted uncomfortably. "Please, I need to talk to you for, like, a second, I promise."

"I don't do talking." He spoke slowly, his voice annoyed.

"If you could just listen—"

"I don't do listening, either."

She seemed to deflate a bit. "Shit. You seemed a lot nicer before."

Jarrod broke out a laugh before he could help himself. "Maybe you've never worked before, but when the people behind the counter smile at you, it's not because they're nice. It's because they're being paid." The sign had cycled back to the flashing DON'T WALK. Cars were already rolling through, holding him hostage to the sidewalk. To her.

"Please, touch my hand."

"Why?" he demanded. "What do you want?"

"It's been two days since I got tipped," she said in a rush. "I need it. Please."

An icy slither worked its way up his back. "Tipped?"

"Fingertips. The girl you were talking to at the counter earlier, you're her friend. You deal, too?" Her eyes searched Jarrod's. "Don't act like you don't know what I'm talking about."

"Someone's off her meds," Jarrod managed, trying to keep his cool. A mortal after Touch. Impossible.

"Look, I know I sound shady as hell. . . ." She hesitated. "I lost my contact. I've been going by word of mouth, looking for a supplier." She wrung her hands.

Jarrod looked closer. The skin was raw, red.

"I don't have any fucking clue what you're talking about. Good luck with that, though." He turned his back to her and crossed the street in a jog.

"No!" the girl yelled in frustration. "You were talking to the girl today, the one with the pink hair. I've been trying to find her." Jarrod whirled around before he could stop himself, people brushing past him. "She can get it for me, then? If you won't?"

He shook his head. "We can't help you," he said.

He could feel her stare until he was in the alley, out of her view, and he waited a few seconds to be sure she didn't follow. The girl was jacked up. Maybe she was a Sider who hadn't figured it out yet. But she'd had a *supplier.*

What the hell, he thought, trying to put the pieces together in any way that made sense. Maybe she'd been in the wrong place at the wrong time too often. Gotten dosed a few times. Maybe someone had been lazy enough that they weren't spreading Touch out over the city. Were there Siders who only passed to a certain mortal?

He left the alley, made it up the stairs to the apartment before he remembered Eden and Az had said they were going out. Inside, he dropped the two extra cups off in the kitchen and then headed back to the living room with his own.

Before he tossed his coat across the back of the couch,

he checked the time on his cell phone. Az had said they wouldn't be late. Jarrod sat on the couch. He'd run it by Eden when they got back.

Sullivan. He tapped a rhythm on his knee. *Could* she have gotten addicted to Touch?

When Eden had still been taking out the Siders, she'd gotten too caught up. Jarrod had accused her of being addicted. His fingers stalled on his knee. Maybe Sullivan was like Eden, able to kill other Siders. Maybe Luke—or Gabe—had found another mortal without a path, made another Sider loyal to the Fallen, the way Libby had been before Eden killed her.

Sider or not, Fallen or not, Sullivan was on her own. *You're not going to help her,* he thought, angry at himself. Last time he'd put his ass on the line it'd been for Libby, and she'd ended up luring them to Lucifer, almost taking them all out.

He stood, pacing.

The pain of his fall from the roof had stopped, but he hadn't spread Touch since he'd taken Luke over the edge with him. Since it wasn't storing up, that meant his body still used it to heal. Even now, he knew his guts weren't right.

He rubbed absently at his arm. But this girl, he was almost positive she wasn't a Sider. That Sullivan was mortal, was—

"Not your problem." He'd let Eden decide. He sighed and rubbed his face. "Seriously need to lose the hero complex."

He thought he heard Eden's voice and perked up. Heard her again, closer, but still in the stairwell. Every second she was less muffled. *Is she running?*

He moved to the door as Eden and Az slammed through it, her eyes wild.

She saw Jarrod, sighed his name. "Thank God you're here."

"What's wrong? Why is your hair green?"

Her arms came up around Az. She reached past him and locked the door as if something would crash through at any moment. "Jarrod, help."

For the first time, he noticed how Az shook.

"Eden, what the fuck is going on?" Jarrod demanded.

She trembled, Az's tremors running through her. "The Bound," she managed.

Jarrod's mouth dropped open. They'd been a threat, but a nightmare one. Distant. "You saw them? Is he hurt?"

Az's legs went out. He slammed his hands over his ears, his fingers digging into the sides of his head as he dropped to his knees, rolled over onto his side.

"No, Az!" Eden dropped, grabbed Az's fingers and pried them away. "He's Falling."

"Shit," Jarrod whispered. He'd seen Az this way

before, in the basement of the building with Luke. Adam had called him and he'd gone, thinking he could talk him down. Jarrod thought he'd been more shell-shocked than mad. And then Luke had shown up, and Adam's eyes had glossed over. And the garden clippers. Jarrod forced away the memories, came back to the present. "What do you need, Eden. How do I help?"

"I don't know." She shook her head, panicked. "We shouldn't have gone. He wasn't this bad earlier." Eden laid a hand on Az's shoulder. "I thought he was better, that it would help him to get out."

"Earlier *today*?" Jarrod scanned the apartment with a desperate hope that something would jump out at him, anything that could help. And then he had it. "This happened earlier and you talked him down, didn't you?" She blinked hard, nodded once. He gestured to Az. "So talk to him!"

She grabbed Az's face in her hands. "Az, look at me." Her voice shook. "You open your eyes right now and you look at me, Az."

Az's head bobbed, almost as if he were drunk. "Get away," Az whispered. "I can't make it stop."

"No!" She grabbed his hand and held their entwined fingers up in front of his face, even though his eyes were still shut tight. "This is me and you together. And I am *not* letting you go." Her other hand grabbed his wrist.

Jarrod shifted awkwardly from foot to foot, not sure whether he should leave, whether she wanted him to hear her saying these things. On the floor, Az hitched a shallow breath.

The trembling stopped. And then a strange guttural chittering came from Az.

Jarrod launched forward and yanked on Eden's shoulder. "Back up." He tightened his grip. "Eden, back up now."

She kept her hand in Az's. "I'm not leaving him," Eden said. Jarrod stayed next to her, ready to make a move if Az tried anything.

"Can you hear me?" she whispered. Az stayed silent and still. She let go of his wrist, touched his cheek. He tensed and leaned into her palm. She turned to Jarrod. "I think he's—"

"So many sins." Az's voice, eerie and mechanical, startled both of them.

"Az?" Jarrod's head cocked to the side.

His eyes snapped open. They weren't covered in the black oily sheen Jarrod had expected. Instead, the colored centers of his eyes were gone. They had turned completely white. Eden dropped his hand, scrambling away.

Jarrod sucked in a sharp breath. "That can't be good."

"Petulant." His smile wasn't natural. It invaded his face, ripping its way onto his lips. He turned his head, and the dead white eyes seemed to train on Eden. "She's a mortal flaw, a wicked taint upon your glory." The smile stretched wider. "The penance is served. Choose. Rise." He nodded twice and shuddered. "Azazel, you are wanted," he screeched. Then the frightened words belonged to Az again. "I'll never go back." He ground clenched teeth. He slammed a hand against the ground, his fingers tightening into claws even as his face relaxed.

Az sucked in a sudden lungful of air as if resurfacing, then fell to the floor.

Jarrod put himself between Eden and Az before she could move. "Open your eyes," he commanded.

Az raised his head, his face pale, eyes their normal blue. They found Eden. She crawled forward as Jarrod moved aside.

"Are you okay?" she asked, reaching for his hand. He latched on like it was a lifeline.

"You sure you're cool now?" Jarrod asked. "What the hell just happened? Your eyes were completely white."

Az sat up. "But that doesn't make any sense," he murmured. He looked up at Jarrod. "Not unless the Bound were . . ." He trailed off. "Sorry, I'm not thinking straight. My head's killing me."

Eden shifted closer to him, almost on his lap, as if he'd disappear at any second.

"You remember what you were saying?" Jarrod asked, not willing to let him get them off topic. Something was going on. "That was Upstairs stuff coming out of *your* mouth, man."

Az shook his head. "I don't know what it was. We saw Michael. He was looking for Gabe."

"Who the hell is Michael?" Jarrod asked. "And Eden said you were bad earlier? What happened?"

Az moved gingerly at first, got his legs underneath him and stood. "I'm fine now. Can we let it go?"

Jarrod opened his mouth, but it was Eden who spoke.

"No." She reached out and let him help her up. "These are things we need to know, Az. Who's Michael?"

"He's . . ." He shrugged his shoulders as if unable to explain. "He's Gabe's. They used to be together. For so long. But then Michael led the charges against me, got me kicked out of Upstairs. He wanted Gabriel to turn his back on me, to shun me. Gabe refused. Michael told me I would only drag Gabe down with me." Az's brow pinched. "I guess I did," he mumbled.

An awkward silence filled the room. Then Eden broke it.

"The things he was saying at the tree, though, he was trying to get you to Fall, wasn't he?" She looked to Jarrod as if for backup before she went on. "And here, it sounded like you were possessed. Can the Bound do that?"

"No," Az said instantly.

"You sure about that?" Jarrod asked. "'Azazel, you are wanted' sounds pretty clear-cut."

"Right, so at the tree he wanted me to Fall and here he wanted me Bound again?" Az shook his head. "I have to decide to go home. I have to want it. The Bound don't fight for anyone. Ever. I would have to choose to go Upstairs for them to not see me as Fallen."

He swayed on his feet, and Eden took his elbow. "The Bound didn't fight for me, and I got thrown out for *love*. Without the wings, and with . . ." He paused. "With what he did, Gabe's not getting a second chance."

Eden helped Az to the doorway of her room. Jarrod followed.

"This isn't about Gabe," Jarrod insisted. "This is about you and what happened and the crazy shit you were saying about Upstairs after seeing the Bound!"

Eden's hand tensed on Az's waist. "Jarrod, let it go. I'm sure it was a weird coincidence," she said.

Jarrod opened his mouth to protest until Eden glanced back at him over her shoulder. The look they shared was the same.

She wasn't buying Az's flimsy story either.

CHAPTER 9

Eden lay in her bed, propped against the headboard, listening. She'd left the door to her bedroom open a crack. Jarrod had shut down the laptop and gone to bed half an hour ago. Az had tumbled onto the couch shortly after. Now, everything was silent.

But are they sleeping? She tucked her phone under the covers to hide the light and checked the time. After midnight. Normally, the apartment would still be active, but with Jarrod's new job and the stress of everything Az had gone through, both the boys were out. She rubbed her neck, refusing to acknowledge how much she longed to lie back and give in to her own exhaustion.

No. She slid quietly out of bed, fully clothed under the blanket. The boys could rest tonight, but they couldn't all afford to take the night off.

Eden slipped on her coat, grabbed her shoes. Before she left, she dropped a pre-written note onto her bed. If

Az came into her room and found her gone, at least he would know she was okay.

She took a deep breath and held it as she crossed the living room, intent on the soft sounds of Az's breaths. They stayed deep and even. She made it to the front door, turned the knob slowly, and wriggled through into the hall.

Scrolling down her contacts list, she yanked on her shoes.

"You're late," Madeline said as the call connected.

"Only a few minutes. You're here?" Eden kept her voice a whisper. Sound carried in the hall, but she knew she was being paranoid. She opened the security door and hung up when she saw her.

Madeline lowered the phone she held. "What the hell are you wearing?"

Eden's skirt rode high up on her thighs, the leggings she wore underneath razor ripped and shredded. Under her open coat, her shirt's neckline skimmed across the top of her breasts, leaving damn little to the imagination. She sighed at Madeline's outfit with disdain. The straight-laced fashion sense bugged her on the best day. Tonight it set her teeth grinding. She eyed the pastel blue top Madeline wore.

"Gabe's Fallen. He's most likely to be in some back alley. Under a bridge. Squatting." Eden started walking down the sidewalk, Madeline beside her. Already she regretted calling, but she didn't dare go out searching alone. The angels weren't the only ones Eden would need to worry about tonight. "The places we look aren't safe. And the people we find there don't take kindly to people in clean jeans and sweater sets."

"Clearly you've given this some thought," Madeline said, sounding impressed. "The problem is—" She hesitated for effect and Eden rolled her eyes. "Why would he be on the street if he could kill someone for their wallet and sleep in a cushy bed?"

Eden exhaled an angry cloud. "He wouldn't do that."

"You don't *know* the Fallen. They con, Eden. They steal and trick and deceive. They want for nothing."

"You said you heard there were complications, though." Eden gave her a sidelong glance. "Gabe—"

"Is one of them. Stop pretending he's not." She shoved her hands deeper into the pockets of her tailored jacket. "Besides," she said, throwing a hand into the air to hail them a cab. "I'll be damned if I'm traipsing into every cracked-out hovel in the city."

Eden ducked into an upscale restaurant, edging past the hostess with a gesture at an imaginary table at the back of the room. She scanned the patrons and shot back every glare from the high-society bitches around her.

After two hours of what felt a hell of a lot like aimless wandering through Soho, it was becoming clear that Madeline's Gabe-dar wasn't as accurate as she'd made it out to be in the cab.

Eden ignored snickers at her clothes as she completed her loop.

"Is there something I can help you with?" the hostess snipped. Eden didn't have the energy to work up a snarky reply. Madeline stood beside her unbothered, fitting in flawlessly.

"Where to next?" Madeline asked before she opened the door and headed back into the cold.

Eden followed without answering. When she and Az went searching, she could almost feel Gabe around each corner, just out of sight, the premonition strong enough to quicken her steps. But with Madeline, there was nothing.

"He's not here," Eden said, defeated. "He's not anywhere." She eyed a small Thai place as they walked past it, but the fight had left her. She didn't go in. She'd hoped. Really hoped this would be the time they'd find him.

"Giving up so soon?"

Eden's head snapped up at the amusement in Madeline's tone. A trickle of unease crept up her spine.

"It's starting to feel like a bit of a wild goose chase," Eden said. She'd called Madeline, hoping she'd help her find Gabe, that the incentive of having Vaughn killed would push Madeline. But with the boredom, the half-hearted attempts at describing Gabe to doormen and waiters while Eden grilled for answers—it almost seemed as if Madeline weren't really searching at all. "It's starting to feel like you only wanted me away from the apartment."

Madeline raised an eyebrow at the accusation. But then the twinkle in her eye caught fire. A devilish grin spread across her face.

"What did you do?" Eden demanded.

Madeline shrugged innocently. "Nothing," she said slowly, drawing the word out.

Eden backed away from her down the sidewalk, stumbling as she bumped into people. Someone shoved her aside. She pulled the phone from her pocket with a shaking hand, only let her eyes flick away from Madeline's long enough to cue up Az's cell. "You hurt them and I'll end you, I swear to God."

The smile dropped from Madeline's face. "Has anyone ever told you that you have serious trust issues?" she shouted as she covered the space Eden had put between them. "I promise, Az and Jarrod are home, safe and sleeping."

Eden glanced up. "I have no reason to believe you."

Her thumb moved to hit Send.

"Wait." Madeline lifted a finger. "How furious would Az be that you *aren't* home?" She dug into her coat pocket, pulled out her own phone and handed it to Eden. "He's *fine*. So's Jarrod."

On Madeline's display was a list of text messages, the same one sent every fifteen minutes since they'd been out. "Apt entrance clear. No lights."

"They're safe and sleeping, Eden." Madeline took the phone back gently.

"You have someone watching?" Eden asked. Her voice wavered, angry and uncertain, knowing how easily Madeline could have had someone send her the texts. They meant nothing. Madeline nodded. "Is there some plan you know about? Is that why you're having them . . . protected? And why wouldn't you tell me?"

"Because you wouldn't see it as me being thoughtful." She lifted a shoulder with a half smile and then sighed when Eden didn't react. "I was flattered when you asked me to help you look for Gabe, and I didn't want something to happen to your boys while you were gone. I know they mean a lot to you."

Eden ignored the attempt at buttering her up. "You're not really looking for Gabe, though. You're going through the motions."

Madeline nodded slowly as if considering it, not answering. "You told me I had to find him before you'd help with Vaughn." She turned to Eden. "I'm asking you to reconsider. Gabe's not meant to be found."

"Not a chance," Eden said instantly. She headed toward the subway entrance they'd passed a block ago. "I'm going home. Call off your goons."

"Stop!" Madeline said with a laugh. "You're overreacting. Let me call you a cab. On me." Madeline gave her a sad smile when she turned around, and then stepped to the curb, her arm raised. When the car pulled up, Madeline gave Eden's address and handed over cash. "You make it very difficult to be your friend, Eden."

"I don't need friends." Eden ripped open the door of the cab and slid in. "One second," she said to the driver before rolling down the window. "What were you going to say earlier today? Before Az got bad? You said Gabe wasn't on a bloody rampage. How did you know that?"

Madeline twirled the end of her scarf. "Luke told me," she said simply.

"You said 'last time I saw him.' It *was* Luke you were talking about, right?"

Madeline snorted. "No, I know exactly where Gabe is. I completely love traipsing around the city with you so I figured I'd keep it to myself." She shook her head, laughing. "Eden, not everyone's out to get you."

Eden stared at her for a moment. "Az and I ran into one of the Bound," Eden blurted. "He had that same angel look. You'll know him if you see him."

Madeline stepped back, the smile falling from her face. "Thank you."

She tapped her hand against the roof of the cab. As it drove off, Eden couldn't help but turn back, the second time today she'd seen Madeline from a rear window. Both times she'd been doing something decent to help. Still, Eden had a long way to go before she trusted her.

CHAPTER 10

Kristen felt her face flush and tossed the covers aside. Underneath, she wore yesterday's dress. She'd come home without a word to anyone, curled up in bed, and let the night slide by in unanswered attempts to call Gabe.

The whispers had started an hour ago, minutes after Sebastian had popped his head in to check on her. She could hear the idle gossip, coming from the room next door. She'd stayed in bed, telling herself to ignore it, that they could have their talk. But as morning waned, so did her patience, their words growing more harsh, brazenly disrespectful.

You know she's losing her mind, right? But really, nobody's surprised.

Her eyes snapped upward to the air duct near the ceiling. She slid the chair out from where it sat in front of her vanity, dragged it against the wall, and climbed onto the seat. Her fingers stretched for the lever that would shut the vent, cut off the metallic voices, their whispers invading her room.

If they'd known she heard them, they'd be terrified of her wrath. Episode or not, it was still *her* home they stayed in, her they depended on for survival.

But confronting them meant she'd have to address the rumors. Without sleep, her brain felt sluggish, too slow to come up with the lies she'd need.

That she was fine. In control.

Kristen slipped a finger behind the tiny lever, knocking it forward to snap the vent shut.

I heard she used to live in a cemetery. What a freak.

Kristen froze. They couldn't know that. Couldn't.

She stood on her tiptoes, bringing her ear closer to the vent. Only Gabe knew about her past. Or so she'd thought.

I heard she has worse secrets. Kristen startled, confused as the voice dropped, darker and breathless. *Ones about the bad angels.*

Her foot slid back in reflex. For a second her toes caught on the edge of the seat, and pain seared through her foot. She slammed onto the ground, her elbows striking the hardwood. No. No. They couldn't know about Luke.

She hobbled to the door, jerking it open. She'd burn confessions from their lips. The door to the next room was closed. She turned the knob.

"You wicked little gossips!" she shrieked, her eyes

flashing left to right. "You know *nothing*."

Silence slumped in every corner as if to mock her. The room held a bed, a dresser, a closet, opened and empty. Unoccupied.

Or so it seemed. They were there, had to be there. She'd heard them.

"You want to play games? We can play games." She dropped to the floor, eyes sweeping under the bed. Nothing.

She'll never find us. Her gaze snapped up. They were still in there. *Shhh shhh!* a girl's voice hissed, and the quiet fell thick as wet snow. Kristen could feel the heavy weight, building on her shoulders.

"You will be so very sorry when I find you," she promised. The pressure lifted a bit with her words. "Do you know what I do all day alone in my room? I plot your punishments. You're all so weak and disorganized. There's no order unless I give it to you."

A giggle erupted around her.

Look at her. She looks like a crazy person.

"I am *not* crazy." Tears burned her eyes and the laugh sounded again, this time from the hall. She glided out the door, cautious and silent. She needed to hear where they were. Find them. Break them into tiny pieces. Her eyes roamed over the walls, trying to pinpoint a location.

Where are we, Kristen? Why can't you find us? Don't you delight in a good game of hide-and-seek? the voice lilted, the teasing tone mocking her in an impression of her own.

"You stop this. You stop this *now*!" They had to be in the ducts. Down the hall a door opened. Her hand shot up, pointing though she kept her eyes glued to the vents. "Get back into your room. This is none of your business." The door closed quickly. "You see?" she said, her voice dropping to a whisper so they wouldn't be overheard. "*That's* control. I'm admired. I'm strong. I keep you all safe. Safe and free from all the chaos, and this is how you treat me?"

Do you think we should tell her? one voice asked the other. She was closing in on them. *She has to know.* Kristen took a tentative step, her head cocked.

Could she really be that far gone?

Well, the other voice answered. *She lost her guardian angel. He carried her mind with him.*

"Don't listen," Kristen whispered to herself. "Concentrate."

Look at her. She's ranting at the walls. Kristen's foot faltered, frozen midair. They were right. If Sebastian found her like this, he'd think something was wrong. *She thinks there are people in the vents.* When the voice spoke again, it didn't come from the vent. Not from the walls. Not down the hall.

I think she figured out where we are, it whispered. Directly in her ear.

Kristen ran.

CHAPTER 11

Eden stared, bleary-eyed, down at the package sitting in the hall, over the threshold of the open door to the apartment. Her name and address were scrawled across the top of plain brown paper, which couldn't be right. She blinked hard, trying to cast away the fog in her brain. She'd made it in without waking Az or Jarrod last night, but the buzz of sneaking out and then back in had robbed her of any hope of sleep. When she focused again, the package was still there.

She shot a quick glance over her shoulder. Az was in the kitchen. She could hear Jarrod's shower running.

A foot-square box wasn't the oddest thing to show up in her doorway, but it made the least sense. Eden and Jarrod didn't normally *get* mail outside of the occasional junk pamphlets for Occupant, and the only personally addressed mail went to the name on the lease—Adam.

Eden's eyes were on the package, but her thoughts

stayed on Adam. He'd been her partner even before Jarrod had joined their group, been more than that before Az had come back into her life.

"What're you doing?" Az grabbed her shoulder, startling her. When she didn't answer, he moved forward, leaning against her, his presence bringing her comfort. She wasn't prepared for the edge in his voice. "When did that get here?"

"I heard a knock," she said finally. "It was sitting here when I opened the door."

"Well," Az teased, "that is typically how the mail gets delivered. Next step is to bring it inside. Advanced lessons include opening."

If she hadn't known him better, the sarcasm would have been enough to have her discounting what seemed to be a tinge of fear in his tone. After last night with the Bound, though, his overly carefree act wasn't working. Something was off. *Why's he sketched out?* He kissed her neck and made a move to grab the box, but she beat him to it.

"And who exactly would be mailing us anything?" she asked pointedly.

"Kristen?" Az offered, but another name took root in Eden's mind.

"Gabe." Eden ripped off the brown paper and slit the tape with her fingernail. With a deep breath, she lifted the cardboard flap.

Bits of shredded paper fell out. She thought about digging through, but wasn't exactly eager about sticking her hand into a mysterious box, contents unknown. Instead, she walked it to the couch and sat down.

Az crossed his arms, standing beside her.

Carefully, she overturned the container onto the coffee table. She poked the tangled strands of newsprint aside. Her fingernail tinked against something. Nestled in the center of the mess of paper was a glass vial, capped at the top.

She looked at Az, uncertain.

"Weird," she said, lifting it to the light. "Is that dirt?" Inside were chalky-looking gray flakes, most of them disintegrated down to a fine powder that filled the tube halfway. Eden's heart sped up. "Oh God, it's ashes."

Az snatched the vial from her. He flipped over the dangling piece of brown paper with the address on it. "No return, but it's not like we need it." Eden raised an eyebrow, not following. "Luke's way of saying hello. Making sure you remember him."

When Eden had taken out Siders, her breath had left them nothing more than ashes. Whoever had sent it knew what Eden could do. The question was intent. Was the package sent to taunt her, because she wouldn't kill the Siders anymore? Was it some sort of threat?

She took the tube from him, staring at it for a moment

before she set it down on the table and wandered to the window. Her eyes fell to the street below, the bit of the front steps that she could make out. "What if he made another like me? What if he's proving he has someone killing Siders?"

"Let him."

She sighed, going back to watching the Siders below. The one who'd confronted her when she and Az had left last night paced the sidewalk in front of her building. "I'm not helping the Fallen. If Luke made someone who will, they need to be stopped."

"So you'll find this Sider and kill them? All you'd be doing is sending them to the Basement. Instead of being tortured, the Fallen will reward them. Like a martyr. A saint."

At the window, Eden went still. "Is that what happened to Libby, then?" she asked quietly. She'd never thought about the Siders she'd killed still existing in any real sense, not with personalities or thoughts. Always pictured Upstairs as a place that absorbed you, took you in. The whole "white light" and all. Now that she actually visualized it, the theory seemed childish, unreal.

"What's it like? Upstairs?"

In the long pause before Az answered, the Sider below crossed the street in front of their apartment complex. Was he giving up on waiting for her? Going back to wherever he came from?

"Complicated," Az said. "I'd tell you, but then I'd have to kill you."

She raised an eyebrow, waiting him out, and after another silence, he finally spoke. "It's a figment of your imagination. Upstairs. I can't describe it to you."

"You can't say it doesn't exist. I mean, you've been there." Her attention drifted back to the Sider. He leaned against the brick, one shoe kicked up behind him. Someone had joined him. They stood, too nonchalant to not be up to something.

She heard Az cross the room. He joined her at the window. "Think about what makes you happy."

You, she thought first, and then a dozen things sprang into her head. Stupid things like coffee and simple things like summer and laughing. The smell the kicked-up ocean gave off after a storm.

"Now what would make Kristen happy?"

The words stopped her thoughts. Her brain struggled to switch gears, flashing back to the crypts Kristen raided for her dresses and jewelry, the strange knickknacks, dried roses, and small monkey in a jar of formaldehyde she displayed on her mantle. The sadistic way she ruled her Siders. Power made her happy. Power and . . .

"Poetry?" Eden offered.

"An eternity of poetry," he said. Eden frowned at the thought. "That. Right there." Az's eyes sparkled. "You'd hate having to read poetry forever, but to Kristen it'd be paradise. Upstairs is the same place, but tailored to each person. Slightly different."

"What was it like there for you?"

She watched outside as the Sider's hand shot out, but it was gloved. He snagged something from the person standing beside him. His glove came off. Eden's own hand touched the glass. She strained to see. The Sider slid his fingers against his companion's as they passed, each heading off in opposite directions. Were they Vaughn's Siders?

"Empty." Az's voice startled her. She'd forgotten her question until he went on. "We were never told we could dream." She turned in his arms. His gaze pierced her, drew her in. "Until I got down here, I never knew there could be more. And now that I know, I can never go back. That place is Hell to me."

"I'm scared." She said it without thinking. Her eyes drifted to the vial, on the table where Az had left it. "Luke's going to keep coming for us. It's never going to end."

His brow furrowed, before the creases faded and he smiled. "You and Jarrod had him crawling away last time. He's afraid of you. How badass can he be, threatening you with a few boxes?"

"A *few* boxes?"

The smile dropped from his lips.

"This isn't the first?" She closed her eyes, trying

desperately to reign in her anger. "How many?"

"Eden, they don't mean any—"

"Az," she said, her voice shaking. "You already lied to me. Don't make it worse."

He swore under his breath. "Five, okay? All the same. Nothing but a pathetic attempt to freak you out. I didn't want you to get upset." He tried to hug her but she raised her shoulder, jerking away.

"I don't need to be coddled!"

A ghost of a cocky grin crossed his lips. "Don't I know it."

"Who's *really* sending them? Michael? Is that what he meant about the smoldering?" She snatched up the vial, rolling it between her fingertips. "He knows the Siders turn to ash when I send them on, so he's what, teasing me? Tempting me?"

"Eden, Michael doesn't know where we live. He doesn't even know where Gabe's and my apartment is." Az crossed the room to the kitchen. The scent of fresh-brewed coffee hung strong in the air. "It's gotta be Luke."

"You should have told me about the boxes, Az," she muttered. It wasn't worth fighting with him over. Not to mention what *she'd* been doing last night. "Luke's going to make a move."

Az took two cups down from the cupboard, then slipped the coffee pot free. She held her cup out to him. "Eden, he's not. And if he was, why wouldn't he wait until we let our guard down?" he went on. "Come outta nowhere?"

She tried to keep the tremor from her hand as he filled her cup. She looked up at him, met his eyes. "Because he wants us to know he's coming," she said. "He wants us afraid."

"Of what?" Az said, trying to reason with her. "What's so scary about ashes?"

Eden sipped her coffee. She crossed back into the living room, heard Jarrod getting ready for work in his room. "Because to a Sider, ashes only mean one thing, Az." She thought of Adam, of Libby, and her stomach tightened in a cramp. "Death."

CHAPTER 12

"Visitor. Counter," Zach said as he passed.

Jarrod tipped back to get a glimpse around a display. He only had to catch a fraction of her hood and black hair to know it was the girl. Sullivan. He pivoted, almost ducking behind the counter before he realized how stupid he'd look. Not to mention it was kind of pointless. Eden and Az seeing the Bound, Az's freak-out—it had him wound up. Paranoid. He looked down at the macchiato he'd finished making and strode to the counter, completely ignoring her as he rang out the customer.

Sullivan wasn't smiling, her face dour. He was pretty sure the black under her eyes had gotten darker. Maybe she wasn't sleeping. Maybe something had happened. She knew about Touch. Did she know about the angels, too? He shot a glance at Zach and caught him looking.

Jarrod leaned over the counter, close enough that only the

girl could hear him. "Look, you can't bother me at work."

"Please talk to me." She sounded totally spent. Looked it, too. She dropped her hands onto the counter between them. Jarrod tensed, thankful Zach was so adamant about wearing gloves. He'd wanted to talk to Eden about Sullivan after work, but it looked like that wasn't going to happen. He glanced back at the clock. Almost six.

"Okay, here's the deal," he said. "You keep your hands in your pocket and wait for me, there." He pointed to the booth at the very back of the coffee shop. "I'm supposed to be off in half an hour. Don't stare. Don't watch me. When I leave, follow me and head left. I'll wait for you a block down."

She nodded and headed to the booth he'd pointed out without another word. He tried not to watch her as he took the next order.

Zach's pretty much permanent smile had taken one of its rare vacations. He glanced down to Sullivan in the booth. "Who is she?"

"Showed up here yesterday, followed me after work," Jarrod answered. "Last night, she asked about Eden and tried to get me to touch her. Want me to get her out of here?" He tried to keep his voice neutral.

"Mortal?" Zach asked.

Jarrod nodded. "Far as I can tell."

Zach's hand tapped against the counter and then

he held it up. "You're off early. Make sure she doesn't come back here. I'll see you tomorrow."

Jarrod snapped off the disposable gloves and whipped the apron over his head. He grabbed his coat from the break room and clocked out. When he got to the entrance, he turned back. Sullivan slid from the booth.

He pulled his gloves out of his coat pocket and put them on. "Later, Zach!" he yelled, and pushed open the door, the little bell trilling.

He turned right out of instinct, but then headed left, further from the apartment. When he looked back over his shoulder, she was hauling down the sidewalk, no more than ten feet behind him now. He stopped and leaned against the brick wall of the building.

She took him in, not saying anything, staring at him. He shifted, and she jumped even as her arm shot toward him, skittish, like she couldn't quite decide whether she wanted to run away or grab him.

"You eat today?" he said quietly.

She shook her head. He rolled his eyes, already pissed at himself as he pushed off the wall. It was pretty obvious he'd be the one buying dinner.

"Come on," he mumbled.

She followed him to the next block. He turned the corner and asked, "You got a preference? We've got Mexican or Cantonese," over his shoulder.

"I'm—"

"Choose," he cut her off. "This isn't charity. I'm buying information off you, and your currency seems to be the edible kind."

She bit her lip. "You're buying, so it should be your call."

"Tacos it is," he said, throwing the door open, holding the part closest to the hinges to give her time to get through. The dinner crowd was in full swing, most of the tables taken, the chatter loud enough that they wouldn't be overheard if they kept it down.

Sullivan went with the cheapest combo on the menu.

"Make it two," he said, slapping his money on the counter. Her eyes locked on his fingers even though they were gloved up. He carried the tray to a table in the back corner, slid onto the seat.

"Eat," he said, leaning back against the wall, pulling his feet up. He folded his arms over his knees, dropped his forehead onto them as she sat opposite him. He waited while she inhaled her enchiladas, not bothering with his own food. When she was done, he dropped his feet back to the floor, crossed his arms on the tabletop.

"All right, I want your story. Details. I'm not going to treat you like I did yesterday," he said. "You know things. I wanna know what."

"But you can get me some Touch, right?"

He watched her silently for a moment before he asked, "Where'd you hear about it?"

"A club with my friends. On Staten Island." She picked at a piece of cheese left on her plate. "I wasn't there the first time, but my friends were," she continued. "We thought someone slipped something into their drinks. They were out of it all night. We went back to try to figure out what they'd gotten."

"Wait, so your friends got drugged and you went back for more?"

She didn't look up from the plate. "I never said I was an angel."

Jarrod raised an eyebrow but the girl didn't see it, and wouldn't have gotten it if she had.

"I got stopped outside the bathroom. I don't know if he overheard us, or I got lucky. Twenty bucks for a dose."

She'd lifted her head, focused on the space over his shoulder. Jarrod pushed the second meal toward her. "Keep talking."

"I got closer to Vaughn after that." She dug into the next plate, took a few mouthfuls, and chewed slowly. She was stalling. Jarrod waited. "He was the one who had it. Who I met the first night. It helped to forget for a while."

He knew what was coming. "Who did you lose?" he asked slowly.

Her attention flicked back to him. "No one to Touch."

She wouldn't look at him, set her fork down on the plate. "Kallie'd had some stuff going on. I don't think any of us knew how bad things were. She never let on."

He didn't know whether he should tell her it was Touch gone bad that took her friend. She hadn't made the connection. A Sider's Touch had cost her friend her life, and here Sullivan was practically begging for it.

"And you took more after?" Jarrod swore, unable to keep the shock from his face. "Jesus. How the hell did you manage to get through it with that in your head?"

She looked up, confused. "What do you mean?"

He hesitated, not sure how much he wanted to tell her. "Well, you shouldn't take stuff while your head's messed up. Dangerous combination. Especially with Touch."

Sullivan leaned back in the seat.

"Listen. I appreciate the dinner. Well, dinners. I just want to get tipped. Preferably without your pathetic attempt at hitting on me. I'm not for sale." She folded her arms over her chest, slumped back with a glare.

Jarrod balked. He felt his face flush. "I wasn't hitting on you. Enchiladas aren't exactly an aphrodisiac." He thought he saw amusement in her eyes, the start of a smile on her lips, but then her scowl deepened. "Trust me, Sullivan," he said earnestly. "You don't want the Touch."

"No? It's not exactly my first time, you know. I was with him for three months."

"With who for three months?"

"Vaughn," she spat, exasperated. "You want info? Fine. He ran all the clubs. The parties. Had quite a few people under him. They talked about your friend. Her name's Eden, right?"

Jarrod nodded, stunned silent by her rant.

"They saw the papers about what happened at the rave. If you could get me a meeting with her, I know I could help you guys out." She dropped her hands absently to the table, her fingers circling her wrists like handcuffs, the skin reddening as she wrung them. "Vaughn had me spreading the word. Marketing. That sort of thing. I could help." Her desperation inched her forward. "I'll work off what you give me. Front me it this one time."

"Jesus Christ." He shook his head. "You're addicted."

He expected her to deny it, pull the "I can quit anytime" thing. Instead, she held out a hand, the slight shake in her fingers almost imperceptible. "Now, do you have it or not?"

"I don't think it's a good idea to hit you up with it right now," he said.

She jumped up out of the booth. "Forget it. I heard someone's got a stash in Queens now."

"No!" Jarrod yelled before he could stop himself. "Um, no, that's an even worse idea." No way could he let her try to track down Madeline. "Wait, who's telling you where to get it?"

She turned for the door.

"Sullivan, stop." He pulled out his wallet. "Twenty bucks to tell me how you knew to find me."

At the mention of the money, her hand paused on the handle, but she shook her head slightly.

"Hey," he said, getting up and grabbing her arm. The momentum spun her. One hand went for the money. The other snapped up to his wrist, her thumb deliberately catching the cuff of his glove. Her fingers wormed inside, slipping across his sweaty palm.

Touch passed, leaving him in a rush, his breath catching, brain panicking. He ripped his hand away, but it was too late. Far too late.

She laughed.

"You don't know how fucking stupid that was!" he yelled.

"Jesus, relax. I'm good for it, thanks to you." She winked and tried to hand him back the twenty as she slipped out the door. He followed her to the sidewalk.

He tightened his fists, the muscles of his arm screaming for action. He used every bit of his restraint not to punch the brick wall beside them. "I don't deal it. It's not a drug, okay?"

"No shit, Sherlock. So much for not treating me like

an idiot." She threw a hand on her hip, taking a few steps back. "Right. Guess we're done here then."

Her feet kept moving, slow at first like she thought he'd give chase. He stared after her, no idea what to do. He hadn't spread in weeks, but he was still using the Touch to heal. Would that make it more concentrated? Less? Whoever had been passing to her had tossed her, and she'd mentioned at least one dead friend. She knew about the Siders, and obviously knew more than she'd told him. And now she was halfway down the block, fading into the crowd.

"Shit," Jarrod mumbled, and then broke into a run. "Wait! Sullivan. Hold up."

She tensed, almost crouched, like the thought crossed her mind to break for it. She looked like she might. "What do you want?"

Jarrod stared her dead in the eyes. "I haven't passed any out in a long time. I don't know if it'll be too strong, or work at all. It could be bad."

"I'm fine. I have a hotel room. I'll ride it out."

"You won't make it through alone." He moved closer. "I could help you."

She looked up. "Why?"

He didn't bother sugarcoating. "Nothing more than personal gain. You shouldn't be addicted like this. I want to figure out why you are. That's it. No catch.

I need you alive to get my info, and you won't be if I don't help."

"What's your name?" she asked.

He paused, realized he'd never told her, that she'd never asked. "Jarrod."

She nodded once. "Jarrod, you are bizarre."

CHAPTER 13

Kristen closed an eye and dusted from lashes to brow bone with a deep maroon shadow. It didn't do much to slow her hammering heart. Luke's show at Aerie would be over by now. She recited half a dozen poems from memory, the cadence of the words soothing her.

After a second layer of mascara, she studied herself in the mirror.

The image was striking. She'd grown used to her thrown-together look, the lack of makeup. Of effort. The fact that she was making the effort for Luke didn't raise any feelings of guilt. This was about false promises of things he couldn't have. Simply playing a game. And if brushing her hair and wearing a tight top gave her an advantage, Kristen would work the angle. Luke didn't have many weaknesses to prey upon.

There were no other options without Gabriel. Already her mind had started to crumble again. She hadn't let

Luke in enough to gift herself more than a day or two of sanity.

And they both knew it.

"If Gabriel would answer his damnable phone," Kristen mumbled to her reflection, one finger stretching her eyelid, applying liner with a heavy hand. *It's been weeks. He knows you're struggling. He must. He doesn't care.* She ignored the voice. "When he finds out how bad he let things get, he'll never leave again." She knew she sounded like a petulant child, didn't care.

Luke, however, had answered her earlier phone call on the first ring.

She stared at herself for another long second.

"Keep yourself together," she whispered to the girl in the mirror. The lips moved along with hers, but Kristen wasn't sure if the girl in the image was acquiescing or mocking.

She lifted her phone from the vanity with a shaking hand, texted Sebastian: "Not to be bothered tonight."

She stabbed Gabriel's number on the speed dial in one last Hail Mary chance.

"Please," she whispered. It rang twice and went to voice mail.

"You're angry," she pleaded into the phone after the beep. "Want me punished? I promise, I'm punished. I'm more sorry than you could ever dream." Her stomach felt too hollow, empty. She softened her tone. "Gabe. Where *are* you?"

She hung up, tossed the phone aside. Eden would have gone after Az anyway that morning. So Kristen had given her every bit of Touch she'd had. And not only for Eden. Because Kristen's first thought had been Gabriel. How much it would hurt him to lose Az to the Fallen. For a bitter moment she wondered what he'd do if he lost *her* to the Fallen.

Kristen pulled her knees up, hugging them to her chest. Deep inside her, things were breaking. *He is losing me to the Fallen,* she realized.

The floorboards creaked softly outside her door.

She slipped off the bed and crossed the room. At least Luke had done her the favor of using the back entrance. She lifted her hand, pressed it against the wood without opening it. From the other side there was only silence. It was her last chance to pull out.

She turned the knob.

Luke stood in the dark hall, his guitar case by his side. She'd been right in guessing that he'd come straight from the show. She could smell the club on him—sweat and smoke and sex—the scents of the crowd.

She staggered back, giving him a stiff nod. He stepped farther into the room and set the black case near the door, then stooped down to unlace his heavy combat boots. He lifted his head as he slipped out of them.

They stood, staring at each other. Luke's smile flared and then faded, a gift he offered only to take away. Everything about him was at ease.

Except for his eyes. Those drank her in with a thirst she wasn't prepared for. "How's it been, my little oubliette?"

"Oubliette? A *dungeon*? You're losing your touch, Luke." She let out a condescending laugh, ignored the flutter in her stomach. "A one-night stand doesn't exactly qualify as imprisonment."

"A one-night stand doesn't typically last three months," he shot back. "You're right, though. The word is all wrong." His fingers, calloused from playing, brushed her hair back, tucking the waves behind her ear. She meant to throw a hand up on his chest, enough to push him back a pace. Her fingers gripped his shoulder. "See, an oubliette is something meant to be forgotten." His hand wound across the back of her neck and pulled her closer. "But I remember every delicious detail of you," he murmured.

Her breath caught, and she dropped her hand from his shoulder. "It's been a year," she said quickly. "God knows you've moved on."

He didn't break her gaze. "God knows nothing."

Kristen shook her head, trying to clear her thoughts. *You're not looking to rehash a fling,* she chastised herself. She took a breath to calm her nerves and then let out a disgusted sigh. "Bored without the blonde? Libby? That's her name, right?" She cocked her head, her tone venomous as she covered her mouth lightly with her hand. "Oops! I guess I should say that *was* her name."

The twinkle slid from Luke's eyes. He went eerily still. "That was business, Kristen. You of all people know sometimes we have to play nice to get what we want." She heard his coat hit the floor and then his body pressed against hers, an inferno. His hands slid down through her hair. His mouth grazed her neck before rising to her ear. "Aren't we here to play nice?"

"Business." Her voice shook. Inside the safety of her pocket, her fingernails cut into her palm. *Don't let him play you. You know how to work him,* she reminded herself. "We're here for business."

"Hmm." His lips hummed again her neck. "So you honestly don't miss us?"

She couldn't move. "It was a lapse in judgment."

"A bad dream you found it safer to forget," he mocked. "You and I? We had a good thing."

"It was a lapse," she repeated carefully, "in judgment."

From her left, she heard a pop, a crackling like a firework on half volume. She opened her eyes and turned toward the sound, confused. Somewhere near the back of her skull, a dull noise started. A flutter of words she couldn't quite make out. The room flexed almost imperceptibly.

"Stop," she whispered.

Luke's hands stilled instantly. The thrill of whatever game they'd been playing, the back and forth, fell away. "Kristen?"

The whispers intensified, a white wall of sound suddenly rushing to take over. Her eyelids fluttered, heat rushing to her cheeks in a panicked flush. She couldn't catch her breath.

"Look at you!" Luke squeezed the sides of her face. "They left you doomed and clueless, and *I'm* the enemy?"

"What are you talking about, 'doomed'?" She tried to focus on Luke, but a dozen thoughts cascaded through her mind. He had to know she was in a tiff with Gabriel, because of her state, but that didn't qualify as doomed. Death couldn't touch her. Neither the Fallen nor the Bound could kill Siders. The Bound didn't even know about them. *Unless they found out,* a voice whispered.

He let her go, strode across the room, and sat on the bed as a terrible thought struck her. What if Gabriel wasn't ignoring her calls because he was angry?

"Clueless about what, Luke?" If the Bound knew Gabriel kept the Siders' secrets over his commitment to them, they'd have him punished. Confined. "Damn it, answer me!"

He patted the space on the quilt beside him. "Sit."

Her unease shifted to dread as she did.

Luke toyed with her rings, twirling them along her

fingers, before he pulled them off one by one. The rubies on her middle finger stuck on her knuckle as they always did. She lifted her finger to her mouth, wetting the ring enough to slip it off. She added it to the pile in Luke's hand. He stripped the bands from her other hand.

"It's been a while since we've played," he said quietly. "You remember?"

She nodded. Each ring worth a question and an honest answer. A game. She glanced down at the pile of metal and jewels in his hand. Five questions, five answers. Luke met her eyes.

"Ask."

She hesitated. He would answer the questions, but he'd be getting his own information from what she asked.

"Do the Bound know about the Siders?"

He took her hand and carefully slid the gaudy emerald onto her finger. "Yes."

She gasped, trying to pull her hand away and stand. Luke held on. If the Bound knew about the Siders, they'd be trying to find a way to eradicate them. *And Gabriel?* Kristen thought, her horror turning to shame. He hadn't called her back because *he* was in trouble. She covered her face with her free hand. She'd thought he was angry and petty, and he was probably worried sick about her. "Let me go."

"No." Luke's tone stopped her dead. His dark eyes glittered like the gems. "We're not done."

She had to use the questions she had left to gain the most information. "Do the Bound know how to kill us?"

"No." Her head tilted in surprise as he slid the ring on. "Ask me how I knew you weren't being helped." He didn't bother with the rings, answered anyway. "You didn't call me in the park. I've been keeping an eye on you, waiting." He didn't look away as he said it.

"If the Bound know of the Siders, they know Gabriel wasn't telling them. He's being punished. And you," she spat. "You waited for me to get sick so you could play games?"

He shook his head, adding another ring to her hand. "He must have suffered so much to keep his secrets. To stay," he said as he looked up at her. "You can't believe he'd let the Bound keep him from you."

She drew a shallow breath, enough air to speak the words. "What have you done to Gabriel?"

"Not a thing. We played the same roles for millennia, he and I, and nothing had ever changed," he said. The gold band was back on her thumb. "No one can force a Fall."

"He . . . No." She yanked her hands from his, stumbling away. She made it to the chair, clutched the back of it. *Get it together*, a voice said stubbornly. *You're showing him all your weakness. He'll break you with it.*

Luke's leg bounced, energy finding its way out. "He confessed. A murder, at his hands."

"It's not possible. There must have been a mistake."

She wanted him to be lying so badly she ached.

It hit her. Sudden terror. Gabriel. Fallen. She couldn't catch her breath, swayed against the chair, her hands clenching the armrest in a death grip. If she could get Luke to say it, smile and say *All a bad joke; I find your gullibility so amusing.* "You swear to me, Luke. You swear to me you're not lying."

"I swear on all that I am."

"I want to see him." She couldn't bear to move.

"Kristen, that's not a good idea. He can't control his impulses. He's unstable." It was written all over his face; he'd say no and leave and she'd never find Gabriel on her own. Not in the city.

"Luke, give me this one thing." An idea blossomed, a desperate, dangerous thought. One that would have broken Gabriel's heart to know she offered Lucifer. She dropped her eyes to the bed.

On the comforter lay the last ring. She held it up.

"Do you know where he is?"

"Yes," he said. She held out her hand and Luke pushed the ring on.

The static of voices had gone silent. A tiny bead of sweat rolled down the back of her neck. "How do I find Gabriel?"

"No ring." Luke's eyes burned black, hungry. "You don't get an answer."

Kristen's heart hammered in her chest. She could almost hear Gabe's voice in her head screaming at her to stop, not to do it. She licked her lips and blurted out the words before she could let him talk her out of it. "If you answer me, I'll owe you."

Luke's irises swirled an oily sheen, a frenzied moan breaking from him. "That's open-ended, Kristen." His tone was a warning, an out.

One she couldn't heed.

"You tell me where to find Gabriel, and I'll owe you one favor."

Luke stared at her for a full minute before he spoke again. "He rides the trains."

"Thank you," she whispered.

"It won't help, Kristen. You can't get him back."

"He made me a promise. I have faith in him."

His laugh sent ice down her spine. "You're better than blind faith. I can help you. Let me take care of you."

She kept her head held high, looked him dead in the eye. "Never."

"We'll see about that," he said, gathering his boots as he opened the door. He blew her a kiss from the threshold.

"Never," Kristen whispered to the empty room.

CHAPTER 14

Judging by the girl scowling on the matching twin bed beside him, Jarrod would be in for a long night. He glanced at the cracked clock radio on the nightstand between them. Three hours ago he'd thumbed the volume all the way down on his phone, turning off even the vibrate. First he'd fix this, get Sullivan through the dose, and then they'd go to Eden. It'd be better to face her wrath than show up with a mortal on Touch.

It'd been four hours. From what he knew, it should have taken effect by now. The real reason he hadn't called Eden, he didn't even want to admit to himself. He wouldn't screw up again. Not like he had with trusting Libby. If Sullivan was a spy and he brought her to Eden, he'd never forgive himself. He had to be sure.

He snuck a quick once-over of her.

"Like what ya see, Tiger?" she asked, her eyes never straying from the television screen.

He felt himself flush. "You feel anything yet?"

"Yeah," she said, rolling over toward him on her pillow. "I feel bored as hell."

He crossed his legs Indian style on the bed. Bored wasn't good. Bored was a first-class ticket to contemplating life, and contemplating life, especially from the few hints he'd picked up from Sullivan about her past, would be a one-way ticket out the window. Quite handy since they were on the goddamned fifth floor. He'd already closed the curtains, unplugged the hair dryer in the bathroom and hid it in the closet, and made her give him her half-full bottle of aspirin.

"So, we'll get unbored. What do you do? Like, for fun?"

She smirked. "I steal Touch from strangers. If it's a super-stellar night, I somehow end up getting babysat by said stranger in my shitty hotel room." After clicking through a few more fuzzy channels, she bounded off the other bed. "I can't sit here all night."

"Where are you going?" he asked as she pulled on her coat.

She reached for his hand like she was going to drag him with her. He had gloves on, not trusting her enough to take them off, but she stopped herself shy and turned away. "Come with me if you want, but I'm going for a walk."

He stared at her. "It's freezing out. And last I checked it was still snowing."

She wrinkled her nose. "Never mind. Stay here if you're going to whine."

"I'm not whining," he said. "I'm stating facts."

"So am I. It is a fact that you asked me what I like to do." Her tone shifted, drifting further from sarcasm with each word until it was almost a dreamy slur. "I like to walk. I like snow."

"Sullivan?" Jarrod uncrossed his legs, standing. She turned to him, the apples of her cheeks blushed pink. Her eyes danced over his, her smile blossoming so bright it seemed to infuse her whole body instead of staying on her lips.

"You care what happens to me." She spun like a ballerina through the center of the room, her gasp full of wonder. "It's true, isn't it?"

Jarrod stalled with a half smile, not sure how to answer. Sullivan twirled away the space between them. Her hand curled across the back of his neck.

Jarrod didn't move.

She mirrored him, holding perfectly still, the grin frozen on her lips—lips close enough to his that he should have been worried, should have been jerking away.

"You." Her fingers flexed against his skin, the word a single breathy exhale. "I want to see beautiful things with you."

He didn't say anything. It was like his brain suddenly decided it wanted to opt out of this one. He barely knew the girl, and she was high on Touch. Plus, it wasn't safe, not with Luke and the Bound both hunting around for Siders now. But . . .

"Okay," he said cautiously. She'd taken the dose good. The worry had melted from her eyes, tension lines between her eyebrows fading. "What kind of beautiful things?" he asked.

She let go of his neck.

"Snow!" she said over her shoulder, grabbing his coat off the bed and handing it to him. "We'll start with the snow!"

She squealed as she reached the door, breaking into a run. He sped up, tearing down the hall after her to the emergency stairs. Her laugh echoed as she slammed through the door hard enough to bang it against the cement wall behind it. The crash reverberated down the stairwell. Her eyes widened to almost comical proportions, her mouth a wide O of delight. "Think they'll come yell at us?"

He turned sideways and hopped on the metal railing. "Luckily," he said conspiratorially, "I'm kick-ass at escapes." He let go, sliding, his legs kicked out for balance. Sullivan bounded past him to the landing and held her arms up like she'd catch him. His hands hit her shoulders, momentum spinning them both in a circle.

This close, he could smell lotion or perfume, her scent summery and wild. Her eyes shot to the exit, back to him. She held out her hand.

"You and me?" she asked.

He looked at her hand, raised his head to meet her eyes. She looked like she really did want him with her. So what if it was the Touch?

The happier she is, the better she'll get through it. He grabbed her hand, working his gloved fingers between her bare ones. Sullivan smiled, stepped back, and pushed the door open.

Just for tonight, he thought fiercely. *Only because it'll help her.*

The crisp air stole his breath as they came out into a back parking lot. Giant snowflakes fell all around them, everything covered in white, sparkling under the domed lights.

She wrapped her arm around his, sticking out her tongue to catch a flake as her head dropped to his shoulder, their steps synchronized as they walked. He laughed, blinking melted snowflakes from his lashes.

"I have an idea," Sullivan said, lifting her head from his shoulder. She untangled her arm. On the snow-covered asphalt of an empty parking spot, she flopped onto her back. A few scrapes and she'd made a perfect snow angel. She smiled at him, seemed completely unaware of the absurdity of lying in a parking lot, giggling like mad. "Your turn!"

Jarrod cast a glance around them, not quite ready to let down his guard. No one. No angels or Siders or mortals.

Only him and Sullivan.

She laughed as he dropped down beside her, flapped his arms and legs twice in a token effort. He sat up and glanced back at the blank spot his head had left. With his gloved hands he scooped up some snow, rolling out two tiny balls. He plunked them down where his eyes should have been.

Sullivan clapped. "Look who's coming around!" she said appreciatively. She added eyes to her own, then pointed at their matching masterpieces. "Our wings are touching!"

Jarrod glanced at Sullivan, only meaning to shoot her a smile, but his eyes wouldn't leave her. Her happiness changed her, brightened her cheeks and eyes, bringing out something in her he hadn't seen before. Suddenly he got it— why she searched out Siders, why nothing mattered more than finding the next hit of Touch. For a perfect second, he got it. Being able to go for it, say what you wanted, live for the moment . . . A rush of adrenaline surged through him.

"Sullivan," he said, his voice wavering. "You're beautiful." Before the words even left him, self-consciousness flared up. "I shouldn't have said that."

The snow creaked, packing underneath her knees as she moved closer. Her arms were around him, hugging him tight.

"Thank you," she said softly. "Why would you say such a nice thing and then try to take it away?"

He didn't answer, wasn't sure what to say.

"You should kiss me." She tilted her head up, her lips brushing against his chin. He closed his eyes, couldn't risk her seeing the disappointment in them.

"I can't." He felt her smile against his skin.

"You can," she said lightly.

"Sullivan, I can't do this." He didn't know what would happen, if it was safe. Eden and Az flashed through his mind. But Az was an angel trying not to Fall and Sullivan was a girl. A mortal girl. A girl whose hands were around his neck, pulling him closer.

And he couldn't pull away.

Her lips hit his. He moaned, the sound surging out of him even as he realized it wasn't because he'd passed Touch, that there was no numb tingle, that it was because of her. He broke out in goose bumps. She giggled and pulled away enough to speak.

"You're cold," she said. "We should go in. To the room."

"I don't think that's—" She held a finger to his lips. He tried to say it again and she kissed him into silence, her finger still pressed between their lips.

Maybe there was nothing wrong with giving in. Just once.

He helped her up, not paying attention to anything but her. "Okay," he said quickly, knowing if he thought about it he'd lose his nerve, lose the moment. "Okay."

They ran through the lot, to the back entrance. A second passed while she fished in her pocket for the pass key and he almost thought he should pull away, but then she pressed him against the wall, her mouth greedy on his, her hand blindly fumbling beside them, slipping the plastic card through the slot.

They stumbled up the stairs, through the door, stripping off their coats, dropping them as their hands roamed, tugged, unbuttoned.

Jarrod grabbed her wrist. "You're . . . Are you?" Sullivan only laughed.

"I'm sure, and I am more than okay." She ran her finger across his waistline. "How about you? Still with me?"

He knew it was partly Touch talking. But Touch didn't make people unaware of what they were doing, just amped up desires already there, hidden away. It cracked open the bottled parts. And maybe, right now, that wasn't a bad thing. He couldn't let her slip away, didn't want it to end.

So he nodded, kissed her again, and let his thoughts stop.

CHAPTER 15

Pedestrians streamed past, slamming into Eden, oblivious to her distress. "He's gone." Az's hand was on her back, comforting her. "Oh God, I can't believe this is happening."

"We'll find him," Az promised. Eden yanked her hands through her hair, searching faces in the crowd.

When Jarrod hadn't answered his phone, she'd told herself not to panic. Talked herself out of checking up on him. Half an hour after he was supposed to be home, she'd called Zach and found out Jarrod had left his shift early, something about a girl looking for Eden. The description hadn't matched any Siders Eden knew, but it had matched the strange girl he'd pointed out at Milton's yesterday.

"Luke has another Sider. She killed Jarrod. I know it." Her stomach cramped. She stopped, leaning against a building. "He'll send me his ashes." Another pain shot through her. "I can't . . . get my breath," she choked out before her throat spasmed shut.

Az's arm came around her hip, holding her up. She sucked in a gulp of air, coughing and blinking hard. Her eyes stung, watering as if they were full of grit, but cleared enough to see Az's concern. "Are you all right?"

She wiped her eyes with the back of her hand, leaving a trail of black across it. She wasn't sure she could get her voice to work without setting off her coughing again, settled for nodding.

"You're going to call Madeline," he said. Before the name fully left him she was already shaking her head, but he went on, wiping her dripping eyes with his thumb. "Call Madeline and tell her what's going on. She's got a whole crew of Siders living with her. She wants you to take out Vaughn. Offer her that in exchange for a search party."

She didn't even know if Madeline would come after last night. But if anything could bring her, it was Eden giving her word about Vaughn. Eden broke into a sob and Az tucked her against his shoulder. "I don't want to send him Downstairs."

"If you had to choose between him and Jarrod?" She tensed, and he murmured soothingly in her ear before he went on. "Eden, you have something she wants. She will help you. Call her."

* * *

Madeline met them in front of Milton's. Within an hour, she'd gathered a list of places where Jarrod was both most and least likely to be found and dispatched her troops. Eden had spent the time silent, sure every moment that Madeline would bring up last night, parts of her warring about whether it mattered. All she wanted was for Jarrod to be found safe.

"You know where Luke hangs out. You'll check those, too?" Az asked.

Madeline shot him a patronizing glare and then pointed past him to the last five of the twenty Siders she'd blazed into Manhattan trailing. "You and you," she said to two beautiful waiflike girls. "Aerie. Get backstage. Check the back lot. Use any means necessary." They left without a word and she went on to the boys, pointing at them one by one. "Stay at Milton's. Jackson, go to the warehouse. Concentrate on the roof and the basement." Eden realized which warehouse she referred to, the one Luke had held Az captive in, and a sorrowful sound broke from her. If Madeline heard, she didn't react. "You," she said to the last slip of a boy. "Kristen's. Take the back stair, check only Kristen's room, and mind Sebastian. Do not get caught."

"Wait," Eden said. "Kristen's?"

Madeline's eyes skipped to Az and back. "I'm being thorough. Kristen's been scarce, and in my book scarce means sketchy."

"What do you mean 'scarce'?" Eden cut in.

Madeline let out an indulgent sigh. "You really hadn't noticed? Scarce. Not present," she said. "And I'm sure it's a silly coincidence, but our villain of interest has also been increasingly off my radar. Makes me all . . ." She made a face, her tongue out to the side as if she'd tasted something gone bad, adding an exaggerated shiver of her shoulders. "Blech."

"You think Luke has Kristen?"

Madeline hesitated, her words careful. "I'd be more worried that she blames you for Gabe's Fall and wants revenge. Then again, she was loyal to Gabe. Perhaps she still is."

"But I never told her about Gabe." The logic gave Eden pause. "You didn't tell her, did you?"

Az paced beside them. "First Kristen and now Jarrod? That's a bit of a stretch to not be linked."

"You've both had a rough night. Look, head home. Take care of her." Madeline's lack of a direct answer drew a frown from Az. "I'll find Jarrod and have him back to you by morning."

Eden grabbed Madeline's arm before she turned away. "Wait. There's something you should know." Her eyes flashed to Az. "I haven't been killing the Siders. I used to." She forced the words out. "Because Gabe's Fallen, my Siders go Downstairs when I kill them. I stopped. That's why I haven't wanted . . . that's why I *can't* kill Vau—"

"Too late." Madeline smiled at Eden's dropped jaw. "I want him dead, and you agreed to make him that way in exchange for a search party. Don't worry; now that we're friends, I'll put some effort into looking."

A sudden pain hit her hard, caught her unprepared, and Eden groaned. Az caught her arm.

"You all right?" he asked. She tightened her lips into a grimace and nodded.

"Get her home, Az." Madeline gave her a pointed look and then took off down the street at a clip.

CHAPTER 16

Jarrod's arm stretched across Sullivan's side of the bed, like she'd just slipped out from underneath it. He wondered what time it was. One, two in the morning? He heard a whispered curse, and then a shuffle in the blackness of the room. He sat up.

". . . can't do this. Shouldn't have . . ." Sullivan's voice trailed off.

The metal of the chain lock clinked as it slid slowly, carefully, like she hoped to slip away without waking him up.

"Sullivan?" he called.

She cracked the door open, and he shaded his eyes in the light streaming in from the hall. She looked back. Her cheeks shone with tears, eyes glistening. She sucked a wet breath.

And then she ran.

He threw off the covers as the door closed behind her and cut off the light. His fingers searched the floor blindly for his pants. He struggled into them.

"Shit," he hissed, forgetting about the rest of his clothes, stopping to yank on his shoes only because he stumbled over them. It was the Touch. He'd dosed her and he'd fallen asleep and now it had gone sour in her mind. He yanked the door open as another farther down the hall clanked shut.

He knew where he had to start looking. A trickle of sweat ran down his neck. He walked to the door for the stairwell.

There's a fifty-fifty shot that there's no roof access, he thought. He had to push himself to open the door. *Another fifty-fifty that I'm wrong and she's not up there at all.*

Floors above him he heard the same clank and click of a shutting door.

"Son of a bitch." He took the stairs two at a time, flight after flight. Sullivan was on the roof. And he was going to go get her.

He made it to the top.

For a long moment, he stared. The tiny plaque on the door read ROOF ACCESS.

When he pushed it, the door stuck, and for a grateful second he thought it was locked, that he was wrong and she wasn't out there. But then it squealed, metal to metal, and shimmied its way open. He didn't give himself time to think—knew if he did he'd never make it—charged ahead until he hit the second door, the one that would open to the roof. This one didn't have a handle, only a push bar. He hit it and was out on the roof before his brain could catch up.

Roof. Terror. Pain. The blast of panic slammed into him. Jarrod grabbed the doorframe, fought with everything he had to keep his eyes open and managed to look up. His fingers clutched the frosted metal, lungs doing their best to suck in the frozen air.

"Sullivan." His voice cracked. She sat all the way at the edge, her legs dangling over. She twisted toward him. He held out a hand, his adrenaline surging. "Careful!"

She went back to gazing at the city she faced, the buildings black shadows with illuminated windows.

"Sullivan, what are you doing? Come away from the edge. Come in and talk to me, okay?"

"I don't feel much like talking right now." Her head dropped, and Jarrod gasped.

"Okay, please, come inside." He stepped forward, hand still glued to the doorframe like his arm was a lifeline. *Let go,* he commanded, but the fingers didn't budge. He yanked loose with a yelp.

Black spots tunneled the outside of his vision. *I'm going to pass out.* The thought sent a fresh rush of panic down his spine. Sullivan tilted her head enough to look at him.

"You shouldn't be out here, Jarrod." Her voice was flat,

cold. He didn't know what to say, how to get her inside. She kicked her feet against the building like a kid on a swing. Jarrod managed a foot closer, sliding slowly, an inch at a time. "You don't even look like you want to be here. Go back inside."

"I don't want to be here." She looked back at him when he said it. "Not going to lie, I'm totally shitting bricks right now." He kept his eyes on her, distracting himself from his feet, which, against every fiber of his being, took him closer to the edge. "I'm afraid of heights."

Running her fingers along the edge of the roof, she scraped up a handful of pebbles, a few loose nuggets of tar paper. She tossed them over, one by one.

"You said you were sure." He took another step forward, wiped his palms on his jeans. "You said you were okay." Her shoulders twitched, but Sullivan didn't answer. "I thought you wanted—"

"I did. What better way to go out, right?" He stayed to the left, finally got close enough to get a look at her face. She wasn't smiling or crying anymore. Nothing. Simply staring off into space, throwing those tiny rocks over.

"Sullivan, this is just the Touch. You know that, right? All you have to do is reach back and grab my hand. We'll get through it, and it'll be over soon."

"Over soon," she repeated, her eyes glazed and far off. A chill crept across his neck. Her fingers dropped to the metal lip running around the edge of the roof, gripping it tight. "Or we could get it over now."

He took a rush of six or seven steps until he was within ten feet of her. Ten feet to Sullivan. Ten feet to the edge. He couldn't do it. Couldn't move.

He sunk slowly to the tar, his chest tightening. The smell hit him, chemicals and dirt and blood. *No.* He took a deep breath. *Not blood. That's over.* He swallowed hard, his mouth so dry his throat felt like sandpaper. Jarrod started to crawl. "Sullivan, talk to me. Look, this is not a road you want to go down."

She shifted, scraped her feet back over the lip. A draft surged up the side of the building and crested, lifting her hair along with it. She turned toward him, just out of his reach as she stood up. Her eyes were wild. "How would you know?"

"Because I did it," he yelled. "And it didn't make anything better. It didn't solve a fucking thing. I lucked out and I got a second chance. But you won't, Sullivan." His voice broke. "You won't."

"I can't go back there." He could barely hear her. "I can't let him find me."

"Back to Vaughn?" he asked carefully, and Sullivan nodded. "Please, take two steps forward. We can talk. I don't want you to fall."

Her lips parted, twitched at the corners. "I came up

here to jump, Jarrod. You do get that, right?"

"No, I totally got that part. Message received loud and clear." He sucked a hard breath, rose onto his knees. "It'd be really awesome if you clue me in on the why."

"Vaughn won't let me go. I can run and run. He always finds me." She nodded, almost to herself. "But not this time. This time I have a solid plan."

"No, you have a shitty plan." He crawled another two feet. "Very bad plan."

Everything that should have been solid felt wobbly, but he managed to get one foot underneath him, trying to stand, before he froze again.

"Sullivan, look at me." He shifted, closing his eyes as he held out his hand, but forcing them open again. He was nowhere near the edge and still he felt like any movement would send him over. "Whatever he did to you . . . Look, I know we just met, so my promises don't mean a thing to you, but if you give me a chance, you have my word I'll help you." He lowered his voice. "He'll never hurt you again."

Her smile didn't reach her eyes, hardly even touched her lips really. Her laugh lurched out, a humorless, lonely thing. "I let them touch me, Jarrod. I wanted them to." Her lip quivered. "But they wouldn't stop." She wrapped her arms around herself. "They'd sneak up behind me and brush my shoulder. The back of my neck. My face while I was sleeping. Any skin. When they gave me too much . . . Vaughn . . . He'd lock me in a room and—"

"You want to quit? Is that it?" Jarrod slid his other foot underneath him, stood, his hands splayed.

Sullivan stared down over the edge. "They wouldn't stop touching me," she whispered. "And now I can't stop wanting more."

"Sullivan, look at me." She shook her head as she brought a hand up to her mouth. "That's over, okay?" Jarrod said. "Eden, she's my roommate; she can help you quit. She's badass. You have my word: you're not going anywhere you don't want to go."

"That's a slippery promise," she whispered as her gaze slid over her shoulder to the parking lot below. She seemed to teeter, and the dizzy rush of fear exploded through him again.

"There is no reason for you not to come inside with me."

"What does it matter?" She kicked, sent a spray of detritus scattering into the empty air inches from her. "Why do you care?"

"I don't know!" he yelled. "But until now this has been the best night I've had in a long time!" He stalled out, the words falling away.

She shook her head, staring off toward the horizon. "Only because of Touch. I'm fun when I'm on it. Without it I'm no one special."

"You're lying," he said. She turned toward him, a flicker flashing through her eyes at the challenge. "I know this isn't the time for pickup lines, but if your options are kill yourself or hang out with me, it would be a serious blow to my ego to not get picked."

She looked down at her feet, up at him.

"One step," he said. She took it, and he let out a half breath in relief. "One more, Sullivan."

Her hand hit his. She dropped against him.

Now, with her next to him, everything suddenly hazed over. Like a terrible trick, the adrenaline seemed to drain out of him.

Jarrod licked his lips. "Listen, I know this is incredibly messed up and ironic considering, but I need you to help me. I have to get inside. Now. I'm gonna freak out in, like, five seconds." A memory slashed through his head. Wind whistling past his ears, the fall, so far, Eden's face above him getting smaller.

Sullivan's arm wrapped around him. "Jarrod?"

"Get me off the roof." He couldn't breathe. Couldn't see. "Just get me off the roof."

She hauled him to the door, grabbed for the handle, and pulled him through. He sucked in a lungful of air, pressing against the wall, sliding down it to the floor, his eyes shut.

"Jarrod?" He heard her fear but couldn't get his mouth

to work to say anything to set her at ease.

"I don't do roofs." His voice cracked, and he felt his face grow hot. "I need a second."

Her fingers ran through his hair, front to back, the motion soothing. He concentrated on the feel of her touch.

"I'm sorry," she said, her fingers stilling in his hair.

He opened his eyes. She stared at the wall across from them. A muscle near her jaw twitched, a frown digging in, taking hold.

"This, right here?" He pointed at the closed door. "This is your rock bottom. From here on there's nowhere to go but up." He stood and took her hand. The last minutes had broken apart any doubts he'd had about trusting her. "We'll go see Eden in the morning, okay?"

CHAPTER 17

Gabe winced, though the light in the hallway wasn't bright. He felt drunk or drugged or both, uncertain whose door he was propped up against until he pulled away and saw the brass letter nailed above him.

He sighed in relief. His mouth was sour, his head pounding, but the door he rested against was his own. The only problem was him being on the wrong side of it.

Another blackout.

"Oh, head, you are *not* happy with me," he grumbled, staggering to his feet. He leaned against the doorframe and waited for the world to steady. He flexed his hands, rolling his wrists in a circle to check for sore muscles. None. He checked his fingernails. No dried blood. *Okay, so you didn't fight anyone.*

His hand shook as he reached into his coat pocket for his key. When he took it out, a business card tumbled to the floor. As he slid his key into the dead bolt, he looked down.

HIVE

the card read, glossy yellow letters against a black background.

COME CATCH A BUZZ!

Gabe bent slowly to pick it up, ignoring the pain in his skull. There was a number, an address on Staten Island. The name held no meaning for him. Had he been there last night? Was he supposed to go there? He flipped the card over. A message was scrawled on the back.

> *A favor for the angel on everyone's naughty list. Watch and learn. Hurry. We're losing them.*

Underneath it, a perfect lipstick print of a pink kiss.

Dull dread coursed through him. He stared at the card. Someone knew him, had found him and gotten close enough to leave the card with him. Or had he taken it himself? A fierce urge ripped through him. Protective. Az. Losing Az? But the card had said "them." Who else?

He closed his eyes, trying to force the memories back.

Who had given him the card? The demons . . . the mortal boy's death. He'd thrown up on the subway stairs and then—

Beats. Thumping bass and lights. A voice, female, familiar, yelling into his ear above the music. "Another mortal path to check . . . forget all about me in the morning, baby." Snippets of conversation. And then part of his own answer. "—would never forget!" Her laugh, a flash of white teeth, pink lips pulling back in a smile. "You're not ready yet. Open your mouth." Bitterness on his tongue. A dissolving pill. "That'll help you get there," she whispered. Her lips hit his cheek. "In and out." Her voice, concerned. "In and out," he promised.

His fingers rose to his cheek, the skin there oily with old lipstick. He let out a frustrated yell, slammed his knuckles against the door. "Come on! Remember!" he screamed, gripping the doorframe. He squeezed his eyes shut. "Come on."

Nothing. The memory was gone again.

He stormed out of the apartment building, yanking his hood up as he covered the block to the subway entrance. He'd go to this Hive place. Someone had to have seen him last night. A bartender would know something. A bouncer. He'd make them talk.

Gabe hopped the turnstile and jogged. Wind stirred through the tunnel as the train screeched into the station.

The few people on the platform pressed forward. He fought his way to a seat at the back of the car, pulling his hood down over his eyes.

Someone fell into the seat beside him.

His eyes flicked over. *No.* He froze, his breath choking off. He fought the urge to look, the need to see her, turned toward the window.

Her. Kristen. Memories flashed through him. Feelings of friendship rose bile in his throat. He ground his teeth, already feeling himself losing control.

Could she have given you the card?

Her gloved hand gripped his arm.

He jerked away. "Don't touch me."

"My God, it's true." She leaned forward, trying to get a look at his face, but he kept his head down. "What have they done to you, Gabriel?"

One stop and he could make a run for it. Before he did something terrible. "That's not my name."

It was true. He wasn't Gabriel, not anymore. And if she hadn't known that, Kristen hadn't been the one to leave him the card. Her voice didn't match the one in his memory.

"It was once. It will be again." She didn't give up, scooting closer, pinning him tighter against the wall as he shrank from her. Already he felt the ice inside, shifting, gathering.

He threw back the hood. "Get off at the next stop." His hand shot out, and he squeezed her wrist hard enough that he felt her bones grinding. Before he could push it away, a smile crossed his lips at the fear in her eyes. "Get up. Get away from me. To the other door." Soon he wouldn't be able to restrain himself. "Please," he whispered. His gut twisted as she shook her head.

"I'm not leaving. We'll find a way to fix this, Gabriel. You helped me for years. Let me help you." He winced.

"You shouldn't have come." His grip tightened, and she hissed.

"You're hurting me!"

He met her eyes. Let her see the malice in his. "I know."

He could almost feel the satisfied pop of capillaries bursting under his fingers. She yanked back, but he didn't break his hold. Defiance kept the pain from her face. Her eyes had lost their look of fear. *How long would it take to break her?* A thrill skittered through him.

"You want to hurt me, fine, but I'm not leaving without you. Talk to me. Tell me what happened, and we'll figure out how to save you."

A memory tickled at the back of his mind. His hands against her temples, the sound of static. He broke eye contact, shaking the image away. "No. Leave me."

"They told me you . . ." She winced, her eyes flicking down to her arm. He didn't loosen his grip. Kristen glanced around the half-full car and lowered her voice to a whisper even he could barely hear above the clacking of the train. "There was an accident, right? And someone was killed?"

"Accident? Is that what you think? Is that what your mysterious 'they' told you?" He laughed, unabashed. "Did 'they' tell you who I killed? What I did?"

She gave her head a pathetic little shake. For the first time she seemed to be realizing he wasn't the sweet innocent Gabriel she'd known. The one eager to cater to her whims. A pissant. A little flare of rage ignited inside him. *No. Control.*

He let go of her arm, held his hands out, marveling over them. "She struggled for her life, even though she should already have been dead. I didn't even choke her." He whispered, his hands tightening into fists. "Just held her under until the last bubbles broke from her lungs. Not a mark on her."

She stared at him in silence, sad doe eyes. He wondered what sound they would make when he plucked them from her pretty head. "You need to leave." Gabe shuddered. "Now."

Her voice barely reached him. "You're not capable of murdering someone, Gabriel. I know you."

"Apparently not so well. I lied to you about it for months, and you never had a clue. You think I don't know why you're really here?" His fingers stiffened, cold. So cold. He had to get rid of her before it was too late. "You still want to let me inside your head?" He ran a finger against her temple. "Do you know how easy it would be to break you?"

She looked numb. "I'm already broken. You fix me."

"Oh you sweet nothing," he murmured. "I'm begging you. Leave before I do something."

"You haven't yet. You won't. I trust you."

He fought for control, thought he heard her call his name. Their eyes met. The connection took. The ice let loose, rolling through him.

Her mind spiraled open, coming undone in delicate tendrils. They drifted around him, through him. So many thin lines, knitting and knotting and choking out her sanity. Her gaze was dead, brown eyes unblinking. He had to make sure she didn't come back, knew there was no saving him.

He dug deep, not healing, stumbled across what had seemed white patches in the static, ones he couldn't see into when he was Bound. He'd been hoping for something he could use against her.

He couldn't have dreamed of better.

"I helped you and you were fucking around with Luke?" He sounded more vicious than he expected, wondered for a brief moment if there was actual feeling behind the words. "You used me to fix yourself and when I wasn't at your beck and call, you went to the one bastard I tried to keep you safe from."

A sob shuddered through her, but no tears fell. "It was a mistake. I ended it a year ago."

"Then how did you find me here, Kristen?" He leaned closer and she flinched.

"I . . ."

Do it. Cast her away. Permanently. "I murdered Eden and I wasn't even Fallen."

"What?" she whispered. One word, brimming over with enough pain to keep him stable, give him time to save her.

"Imagine what I'm capable of now," he continued. "Get out of my sight. If I see you again, I won't hold back."

The train shuddered into the station. Kristen stood, locked eyes with him as she staggered backward, out onto the platform, her head shaking slowly. And then she was gone.

Gabe doubled over on the seat, dropping against the cold metal wall of the car. Sweat broke across his brow. For a moment he thought he'd get sick from the loss and guilt rolling over him. Not his. No, they had to have been remnants left behind by Kristen.

The only thing he could do to help her was to send her away. He'd done it. Held his ground. Didn't hurt her.

Pride swelled inside him until he remembered the look in her eyes.

The pain.

"Doesn't matter," he assured himself. The important thing was that she was okay, holding her own. Still strong.

CHAPTER 18

Sullivan hadn't said much. They walked fast, covering the ground between her hotel and the apartment in fifteen minutes. He kept wanting to ask her if she was all right, but it seemed sort of stupid. She'd almost jumped off a building.

He glanced down at her, trying to think of something to say, and settled for putting his arm around her. For a second she tensed and he thought she'd shrug it off, but she didn't. He could feel her shaking, even through his thick coat.

A two-block straight shot and they'd be at the apartment. He'd been cautious, taken a few extra turns when he'd noticed a guy walking their same way for more than a block, not wanting to ask her what Vaughn looked like and scare her. Definitely not wanting to run into the Bound, but unsure what any of them looked like. The Fallen hadn't bothered them since the roof, minus the few boxes that had come for Eden.

No one seemed to have followed them.

He glanced at Sullivan again, watching her face. He'd seen glints of things in her last night, determination and adventurousness that he envied. The Touch had brought them out, but if she didn't kick the habit, it would also be what killed them off. She'd been so close to going over the edge last night. What if he hadn't woken up?

She looked up and caught him staring. "Don't look at me like that," she said, cold enough to break the mood.

"Like what?"

She sighed angrily. "I don't know. Like I'm going to take off on you."

He shook his head. "I was thinking about how you were last night. Like how you just decided you wanted to kiss me and went for it." She tensed, but he went on. "So I think if you wanted to take off, you could." They were getting close to the apartment. He took his arm from her shoulder and pulled out his keys. "I also think if you wanted to quit Touch, you could do that, too."

She looked up at him in surprise. Her lips parted, but she closed them a second later so he leaned forward and kissed her quickly.

"We're almost there," he said.

Jarrod noticed the two Siders on the stairs. He led Sullivan past them up to the security door, his key ready.

"Hey, man," one of them said. "She's going to start coming out again, right? If we wait?"

"No." He kept his voice firm, slipped his key into the lock. He had Sullivan go through first, wanted her out of their sight. Jarrod closed the door behind them, making sure it latched. He didn't think anyone knew what apartment they were in but could only imagine what would happen if the Siders started knocking on the door instead of hanging out front.

"They're waiting for your roommate?" Sullivan asked, glancing back out the window next to the door. A face pressed against the glass, watching them. Suddenly, Jarrod realized how much he hadn't told her.

"For Eden. Yeah." As they climbed the stairs, he kept his attention on the keys, fiddling with them until he separated the apartment key. "Look," he said, turning to Sullivan when they reached the door. "Whatever happens in here, keep it together. Play it cool. I promise I'll tell you everything after, okay?"

He should have warned her. At least dropped some hints. *Oh, like what?* he thought miserably. *Hope you've got a thing for necrophilia?*

She leaned against the wall as he put the key into the lock. He didn't have a chance to turn it before the door flew open, yanked away. Eden threw herself at him, squeezing tight enough that his ribs felt like they were cracking again.

"Jesus Christ, Jarrod. Where the hell have you been?" she demanded. She pulled back, her expression darting from rage to relief. Her eyelids were swollen and pink.

"You're not . . . the Bound . . . ?" She seemed to force herself to take a breath.

Guilt flooded through him. "Oh God, Eden, I'm sorry. I wasn't thinking like that."

"You're okay?"

"Yeah, I'm fine!"

Her eyes blazed. "Then why the *fuck* didn't you answer your phone!" she yelled, throwing her hands out. Eden finally noticed Sullivan and fell silent, the last of her words echoing through the stairwell, fading.

Sullivan had taken a stride away from the door, lowered a foot onto the step below their landing.

"I'm sorry," Eden said, her tone even. "I didn't realize you had a friend with you."

She stared, sizing her up, but Sullivan didn't break.

"Eden, this is Sullivan. Sullivan, Eden," he said carefully. "She's not normally so hostile right off the bat," he added, hoping for a break in the tension. Neither of them smiled.

He shifted closer to Sullivan, put his hand on her back. "I brought her to talk to you."

From behind her Jarrod heard footsteps crossing the apartment. Az came to the door.

"What the hell, man?" His eyes skipped across the tense standoff, settled on Sullivan. Jarrod saw a flash of something cross his face, his mouth opening, closing like he thought better of whatever he was about to say. Which was fine with Jarrod. Eden was enough of a challenge.

"Do we have to do this in the hallway?" Jarrod asked. Eden crossed her arms over her chest, leaning on the doorframe. Half a minute passed before she stood aside.

Jarrod whispered to Eden as he passed. "Mortal. Doesn't know much about us." Eden nodded, her brow pinched in uncertainty.

Az dropped onto the couch, his glare menacing. "You ever do anything like that to her again, you and I are going to have issues, understand?"

"I'm sorry. I wasn't thinking." If Eden had been as upset as he imagined, Az had had to watch her that way. Jarrod wondered if he'd struggled with the Fall again. Jarrod headed for the kitchen, but Sullivan slowed until Eden caught up, as if she didn't want Eden at her back.

The table, pushed in the corner, only had two sides open for sitting. Jarrod tapped a chair and Sullivan dropped onto the seat. He took the other, tipping back and balancing on the legs.

"She was at Milton's the other day," Jarrod started, the pad of his thumb tapping out a nervous rhythm on his knee. "I pointed her out to you."

"I remember," Eden said.

"I got off my shift yesterday. . . ." He hesitated.

Sullivan snapped up. "I waited for him and I stole Touch. He stayed with me last night to make sure I didn't crash and burn."

Jarrod's shoulders slumped. "Shit."

Eden stopped pacing. "How do you know about Touch?"

Jarrod tipped forward, the chair legs striking the floor. "They're selling it. Like a drug. Sullivan was dating the guy who runs Staten Island. Eden," he said, looking up, meeting her wide eyes. "She's addicted to Touch."

The refrigerator hummed.

Eden spun suddenly on Sullivan. "What're you after?" she demanded.

Sullivan shrugged. "I don't know what you mean."

"Oh, that's convenient."

Jarrod scoffed. He'd expected drama, but this was getting ridiculous. "Come on, Eden. You're pissed at me, not her."

"She's not one of us. You had no right to bring her here. We've played this game before, Jarrod."

He stared her down, his head shaking slightly. "It's not like that," he promised.

"It doesn't even look slightly familiar? Don't you remember the last damsel in distress you helped out?" Eden leaned forward as her voice raised, seemed to catch herself as she realized how close she was to Jarrod. He froze, didn't dare inhale. She tipped her head to the side, careful of her breathing, but her rage didn't dissipate.

"Yeah," he said, catching her eye, holding it. "Before Libby, the last 'damsel in distress' I helped out was you, Eden."

"Look," Eden said, turning to Sullivan. "Did Vaughn send you here?"

"How the hell do you know about Vaughn?" Jarrod cut in. Eden held up her hand to silence him. He turned to Sullivan, unsure what to do, how to react. *Did I do it again? Put us all in danger?* Doubt filled him.

"No, I wasn't sent here." Sullivan picked angrily at the edge of the tabletop. "I heard about you from Vaughn before I took off. I needed Touch. When I figured out Jarrod worked at that coffee shop, he was easier to get to than you."

He couldn't help the hurt sound that came out of him. Sullivan's head shot up. She held his gaze but said nothing.

"So that's it?" Eden said. "You used him for the Touch?"

"I never said that." Sullivan blushed, unconsciously reaching for his gloved hand. He didn't pull away, but dropped his eyes, embarrassed. Eden didn't need to know what they'd done last night. "It started that way."

"Yeah, I'm sure by now you two have made a real connection. But that," Eden said, pointing at their hands, "is way more complicated than you know."

Jarrod cocked his head, his anger flaring back.

Next to him, Sullivan unlaced her fingers from his and crossed her arms near her waist. "Yeah, the whole him being dead thing does complicate the issue a bit."

Jarrod's mouth opened but no sound came. He closed it again, turned to Eden. She stared at Sullivan in shock. Jarrod followed her line of vision back.

A small, almost victorious smile tipped up the corners of Sullivan's lips. "I saw Vaughn get shot at the club. Three times smack-dab in the chest. He tried to play it off like the bullets only grazed him until I saw the holes. After that, he had to explain things."

She knew. The words jumped around in his head. She knew and she'd known last night and hadn't cared. "And you were, what, fine with him being . . . ?" Jarrod faded off in disbelief.

"What, dead? Of course not! I flipped. Complete catatonic freakout mode. But, I got over it." She dropped her eyes. "I mean, I thought I was in love with him." Her eyes darted to Jarrod, then away. "Before I left, I heard him talking about you, Eden, where you hung out, so I came here hoping he wouldn't."

"What exactly do you want, Sullivan?" Eden asked.

She swiped a few strands of black hair back from her face. "I didn't know what I was getting mixed up in with Vaughn." She glanced down. "With everything," she added, quieter. "On the way over here, Jarrod said something about being able to quit." She took a slow breath. "If I did want to quit Touch," she said as she looked up at Eden, "would you be able to help me?"

For almost a full minute, no one spoke. Eden stared at Sullivan, her face unreadable.

"Jarrod," Eden said finally. "Living room."

They headed in that direction, found Az sitting on the couch. Jarrod wondered why he hadn't come into the kitchen with them. Maybe he was worried the fighting would set him off. The look he gave Jarrod wasn't exactly friendly. Eden walked them past him, heading to Jarrod's room. He closed the door behind them, but Eden kept her voice low anyway.

"You believe her when she says she's addicted?"

He didn't even pause to consider it. "Yup."

"What happens when she doesn't get it?"

"Didn't ask her." He shrugged. "But she looked pretty bad at Milton's, didn't she?"

Eden asking questions was a good sign. It meant her curiosity was piqued. That she wanted answers.

She pushed up her sleeves, her bracelets jangling. "Find out. You're in charge of her, Jarrod. I don't want her out of your sight." He nodded, managed not to smile in relief. "If she got out of Staten Island before Vaughn's little drug ring was broken up, she left right before it happened." She paused. "Otherwise, she's lying and she was sent here. Find out what she knows. If Vaughn's pissed off enough, he might have sent her to see what it would take to get me to work for him, take out the people who stepped on his toes." She kicked absently at the base of the door. She shook her head. For a second he thought she'd go back on letting Sullivan stay. "Last night, Jarrod. I couldn't find you. I thought Luke had you."

"Eden."

"I needed people to look, so I bartered with Madeline. Her Siders searched for you."

"In exchange for what?" he asked, suddenly on edge.

She looked up and met his eyes. "In exchange for me killing Vaughn."

"Shit," Jarrod whispered. "You can't do that, Eden."

She shrugged. "I already said I would. If Sullivan is on the run from Vaughn, I don't want him tracing her back to us. To me."

"Where else is there? I don't think Sullivan could take Kristen's . . ." He tried to find something specific but couldn't narrow it down to one. "Well, Kristen in general."

"We're in agreement there." Eden tapped a finger

against her lips. "Az and Gabe's apartment? He said the lease is paid up through the end of the year."

"I don't like being split up. The Bound are around, and Luke seems like he doesn't want us forgetting about him, either." Jarrod crossed his arms over his head, his hands gripping his elbows. "Eden, I know you trust Az. . . ."

"Don't."

"He freaked me out. Those white eyes." He turned back to her. "One of these times he's not going to come out of it."

"You didn't seem to care last night." A moment passed, Jarrod's shame keeping him silent. Finally, Eden relented. "Az is fine. Madeline's going to work on finding Gabe. Until she does, he has me. I'm meeting with her tomorrow, so I'll run this whole addiction thing by her, see what she says."

Jarrod leaned against the door, unwilling to let it go so easily. "If you're sure."

"I am," she said, but there was a waver in her voice he didn't like. The look in her eyes told him fighting about it wasn't going to get him anywhere yet. She was still too angry at him for taking off last night.

"Then I'll hole up with her at the apartment. You promise me anything goes on with him, he even looks funny, you call me."

"I promise."

Jarrod opened the door. Before he passed back into the living room, Eden spoke.

"You just met her, Jarrod," she said. "I know you want to help her, but my advice? Don't get too close."

"I'm not," he insisted, but he couldn't help dropping his eyes.

CHAPTER 19

Kristen crossed the street to the cemetery and climbed over the iron fence with ease, the footholds long since memorized. The weight of the past hours pressed her even lower as she hit the ground. Gabriel. She gripped tight to the thick material of her coat below her neck, an oversized button jabbing into her palm. She wished she could crack open her chest, fill it with the unfeeling granite of the tombstones peppered around her.

Gabe's words skimmed through her mind even as her eyes skirted across the gravestones: *held her under until the last bubbles broke . . . lied to you for months . . . Eden . . .*

Betrayal after betrayal after betrayal. *How could they keep something like this from me?*

She straightened and kept going, one foot in front of the other, her footsteps crunching through the snow. She didn't glance up as she walked, knew the tombstones well enough to turn left after Olson, pass the obelisks for

Bennett and Adrian. Finally she slowed, then stopped. Kristen raised her head.

One of the stained-glass windows had been covered over with plywood, now warped enough that it peeled away at the corner. The heavy oak door was shut, but she knew it had no lock. Kristen opened it slowly.

The gray winter light streamed in the windows. The center aisle led between four rows of half pews to an old wooden crucifix hung on a beam, an empty candelabra resting to the left. There was no pulpit. It could barely be considered a chapel.

She considered it home once.

Those visiting the cemetery didn't often venture so deep, and if they did, assumed the chapel was a mausoleum. The building had no heat, no electricity, but the steady stones cut the wind. Kristen canvassed the room in case another soul had stumbled upon it, used it for shelter. The chapel was empty.

Her heart sped up, the scents too familiar, dragging up memories of loneliness and struggle. Everything looked the same. Kristen sat, the cold wood of the pew leeching into her thighs. Though she'd been to the cemetery dozens of times, she hadn't been back to the chapel since Gabriel had found her, rescued her.

You're wasting your time, she thought, licking her lips. *It's not going to work.*

She cast her eyes up to the crucifix hanging above the altar.

"Hello." Her voice broke, too quiet. She started again. "This isn't a prayer, but Gabriel said sins need to be spoken, so maybe someone's listening." She yanked the cuffs of her coat down past her wrists. "He needs your help," she said quietly. "He's in trouble. Something terrible happened and Az must have tricked or coerced him and I think Gabriel made a terrible mistake." Her words flowed faster. "And now his punishment is . . . I can't see how any of this is helping anyone and if you could—if you could give him another chance." She stopped, her chest heaving. Gabe had killed Eden. Because Az was too pathetic to do such a horrible thing himself.

Rage built inside of her. They were there on that roof. They could have helped him, protected him, and didn't.

They'd kept it from her. Worse, they'd left Gabe to struggle on his own, let the wicked parts of him chip away until there was nothing left. She raised the back of her hand to her mouth, stifled a sob.

If she'd been able to get to Gabe sooner, she could have helped. Instead he'd sent her away, the look in his eyes evil enough that she trembled even now, a dirty, watched feeling creeping over her. Gabriel was gone.

"No." Kristen laced her fingers together on the pew in front of her, head bowed, her words coming with renewed vigor. "This part *is* a prayer. Please," she whispered. "Please help him. Tell me what to do and I promise you, I'll get him back to you."

The chapel stayed silent and still. She felt nothing, no presence, no heavenly light. She wasn't sure what she expected, felt more foolish as the seconds ticked away.

Kristen dropped her head onto her hands and rested it for a beat before she straightened, brushing the tears from her cheeks. "God help me for what I'm about to do," she whispered, knowing the words were worthless.

No one was listening.

She pulled her phone from her pocket and called some-one who would.

When he answered, Luke's tone was victorious. "Did you see everything you needed to see?" he asked. "If so, I have an offer."

"I'm ready to talk," she said quietly.

"Where would you like to meet?"

"Somewhere discreet." She could hear the smile.

"Why, Kristen, are you embarrassed to be seen?" *With me*, she waited for him to finish, but the words didn't come. The uncomfortable silence thickened, as if the question wasn't rhetorical, as if he expected an answer, before he continued. "My place would be fine."

"Time?" she asked.

"At your convenience."

Kristen saw no point in delaying. "Now."

"I'll be waiting."

She slid the phone into her coat pocket. *You'll do this because you have to,* she told herself again.

Just until I can get back to you, a voice whispered. For a moment, she was sure it belonged to Gabriel, wasn't merely in her head. But Gabriel was gone. Gabriel had risked everything for Eden.

For Eden.

Not caring that he left Kristen behind, no more than collateral damage. Kristen closed her eyes. *Do not trust the Fallen,* she reminded herself. Gabe was one of them now. Her Gabriel was gone. Luke would help her, but only because they'd started a game they'd never finished. And now he held the full deck.

Her brain hummed, the elevator groaning the way she remembered, metal scraping metal as it passed between the twelfth and fourteenth floor. The building skipped thirteen, but the elevator never let it pass by so easily. The chill from the chapel didn't leave her, feelings of déjà vu clinging to her like spiderwebs, growing thicker as she approached Luke's apartment. There was a seedy element she remembered so well, the gut feeling that getting caught wouldn't be worth the indiscretion. The door opened before she had a chance to knock.

Luke cocked a hip against the doorframe. "It's good to have you back," he said.

She strode past, draping her coat over one of the bar stools tucked up against the island that split the living room and the kitchen. "I am not *back*. I'm here to barter," she snapped.

Luke leaped over the back of the couch, the cushion creaking as he landed. "No, I'm afraid that won't do. Come sit."

Kristen assessed the room. She could sit on the floor, but that put her below him. The chair cowering in the corner would make it obvious how little she wanted to be near him. Luke's eyes sparkled at her hesitation. He patted the couch. "You know I don't bite."

Kristen moved slowly. "You have an offer. I'd like to hear it. No commitment," she said, sitting next to him. The leather of the couch was cold.

"Commitment. Committed." He met her eyes. "Odd choice of phrasing."

"Only odd that you'd be callous enough to call attention to it," she scoffed, crossing her arms over her chest. "Or perhaps not odd at all now that I think about it."

He clucked his tongue as if taken aback, though she knew her words had no effect. She wished she could say the same about his. She knew what she must look like. Tangled and forgotten. She sighed, giving him what he wanted, her helplessness. "You know how I am, and how I will be, and why I have no other choice. Tell me the deal, Luke."

He stood and pointed toward the kitchen. "I'm going to grab a drink before we get into things. Would you like something?" he asked. "Cola? Juice? I have anything you could want."

"I'm sure you do," Kristen mumbled, then raised her voice. "No, thank you."

Luke clasped his hands and walked into the kitchen. Kristen took the opportunity to look around more closely.

The apartment hadn't changed much. The soft leather of the furniture dulled the sharp lines of black trim. A flat-screen television took up most of one wall. A picture window looking out over the city took up a second.

Kristen meandered to the window. Below, headlights trailed through the early evening. The sun had dipped behind the buildings. She held her hand against the glass, a ghostly outline blooming around it. From behind her came a soft swish. Her fingers smeared through the fog as she turned, expecting Luke, finding nothing.

In the kitchen, ice clinked into a glass. And then, softer, nearer, she caught a rustling of faint whispers like bird wings.

"Ignore it. It's not real." Her heart sped up anyway.

Luke came back into the living room. *Superb timing,* she thought. He'd probably been waiting, caught the scent of her fear.

"I brought you something," he said, raising one of the tumblers he carried. "You looked thirsty."

She took the glass, the sides of it slippery with condensation. Inside was a yellowy pink fluid, speckled with misshapen clots of red trailing membranes. He raised his own glass to his lips, slurping down one of the clots with a wet smack.

She almost retched, swallowed a throatful of bile. He caught her expression and lowered the drink.

"Strawberry lemonade?" he said.

She glanced into the glass again. A piece of berry had made its way through the ice and floated on top. Crushed strawberries. Nothing more. Luke's laughter echoed in the glass as he drank.

"Of course." Her words were clipped. The lemonade was tart and cold. Her head seemed to clear as she swallowed. *Stay calm*, she told herself.

"So where were we?" Luke asked, plopping back down into the corner of the couch, an arm thrown over the armrest, dangling the glass comfortably. "Ah yes," he said. "You were avoiding my question as to your mental well-being."

"Which I intend to continue doing." Kristen sat on the couch, careful to keep her distance.

Luke raised an eyebrow. "Well then, what shall we talk about to fill the awkward silences? How your precious

Gabriel is faring? Or your new best friend, Eden?"

Kristen took a deep breath, held it. She kept her eyes on the floor, her voice sharp; the perfect mix of demure and obstinate. "What do you want me to say?"

"You found him, I take it. Did he tell you what he did?" When she didn't answer, he went on. "It couldn't have been easy to hear. How are you?"

Kristen shot him a glare, shaking her head slowly. "I found him. I don't need your sympathy, so spare me the theatrics."

"I deserve credit, especially since it's so rarely due. You thought I was lying about him." The ice clinked in his glass as he set it down. "I have never *once* been dishonest with you, have I?"

She hated the rush of blood to her cheeks.

"Have I?"

"No," she whispered.

"You need me? I am there. You want me to back off? I back off." His hand rested on the cushion between them, closer to hers. "I do everything to please you. Even now, you've come here only because I'm of use to you. You're using me. We both know it and yet, I enjoy your company."

Kristen held tight to her mask of nonchalance. "You make me insane."

He laughed. "That is delightfully ironic." He reached out and ran a fingertip across the rings gathered against her knuckles. "You know you need me, don't you?"

She opened her mouth to respond, but a rustle caught her attention. The same one as before. She tilted her head, her ears tuning in to it. *Birds?*

"Kristen?"

The sound untwisted like a spiral; she could almost see the swirl of air. Darkness rose behind it. The wall started to crack, plaster crumbling from the corner, revealing exposed beams.

"What's happening?" Kristen whispered. A tearing noise echoed through the room, like an animal ripping through the cracks. Panic rose in her throat. "Luke?" She jumped from the couch, her eyes darting around the room.

A wet, leathery wing slapped against her cheek. She shrieked and smacked it away.

Luke's hands cupped her face. "Whatever's scaring you, it's not real."

She couldn't catch her breath, could almost see the things now, shadow bats, blurs of air. Something scraped her skin. She pressed against Luke, each word a separate gasp when she tried to speak. "They're. Touching. Me. I can feel them."

"What is?"

"Bats. They're bats." She *could* see them now, streaming from the hole in the corner, from the rafters.

"It's winter," Luke said softly. "Wouldn't bats be in hibernation?"

She gulped.

"I can make them go away." He stared at her, his eyes unnerving. She blinked hard and fast. Luke gripped her upper arms.

"You. You're doing this?" she got out.

Luke sighed in frustration. "You're having an episode." His fingers wound gently around the back of her head, massaging into her hair. "I can help, but you have to let me."

She focused tightly on his words, buoys keeping her afloat. "Don't you see them? You can't feel that?" she whimpered.

Luke pulled her in, his forehead dropping against hers. She had nowhere to look but his eyes, the deep brown melting into her like liquid ice, filling her. She blinked away a snowflake, felt it drip down her cheek. *No*, she thought. *Tears*. Only tears. Luke's eyes muddied, a mix of emotions she couldn't place, quickly darkening back to normal. "Kristen. Now," he demanded. "Please."

"Yes!" She choked it out, a final plea before she drowned in her fear.

"Don't close your eyes," he said.

He squeezed.

Screaming lines of sound rushed through her skull like a current toward Luke's hands at the back of her neck. Her vision tunneled. The pitch rose, glass-shattering frequencies whizzing past the insides of her ears. Burning, sizzling sounds, dizzy tightness. Kristen gasped, the pressure turning to pain.

"Almost there." Luke's voice found her through the cacophony. "Hang on for me."

She clutched his wrists. "Luke, it hurts."

"Now," he said.

His fingers dug a line up the back of her head, each fingertip feeling like a splash of frigid water. Her ears popped as the pressure released. The pain burst and broke open, faded.

Silence.

Blessed silence. Luke brushed her hair back, surprisingly gentle. His breaths came heavy. "Better?" he asked.

He gave her a moment to answer, took her elbow when she didn't and helped her to the couch. She fell back against the cushions, suddenly exhausted.

"The pain is gone?" he tried again. She nodded, doing everything she could to keep the tremble from her lip.

"It was different with Gabe," she said quietly. Gabriel had carefully untangled her mind as he slowly worked; she would have given anything to feel that care again. Luke jerked everything tight and sheared it loose. She didn't want to think about damage.

"I hate this," she whispered. She sounded like she hadn't slept in days, but her brain felt sharp, clean. She felt untainted for the first time since Gabe had Fallen. *Ironic*, she thought bitterly.

Kristen closed her eyes. A moment later the faucet turned on in the kitchen. The sponge squeaked against the glasses Luke washed. She waited, but he didn't speak. She couldn't be sure, but part of her wondered if he'd given her the moment to recover.

The water shut off and she heard him coming back. "Why *did* you come that first night to see me play? You knew who I was."

The memory of badass incarnate in leather and an electric guitar drifted over her. She wasn't prepared for the light skip in her stomach.

"I've always known about you." She opened her eyes, turned to look at Luke. "I came because he left me." Gabriel's reputation didn't matter anymore, not that Luke would care anyway. "He wandered away like I thought he'd done this time. He always told me to call if I needed anything, but then sometimes he wouldn't answer. Sometimes he made me feel like such a burden. I was feeling . . . spiteful, I suppose, and dangerous." She gifted him a small grin as he sat beside her. "And you're about as dangerous as they come, aren't you?"

He laughed, pulled a knee up and balanced his chin on it. "That night."

He shook his head, lost in the memory, every moment

of their meeting etched in her own mind.

After the show, Luke had come toward her, his flock of groupies surrounding him like cliché imitations of harlots feeding grapes to a Roman god. Kristen alone hadn't joined in on the worshipping. He snapped up the water bottle one offered, then cracked it open and drained it. Brushing away the girl's hands with a smile, he had turned to Kristen.

"You," he said, pointing the empty plastic in her direction. Kristen had raised an eyebrow at the possessive glares from the girls that clung to him. Luke strode forward, shaking them off like a cloud of gnats. "Who are *you*?"

"Me?" She'd slid off the stool, taking the first few steps toward the door. "I'm busy."

The girls around him had gasped. Luke's head had tilted, as if not quite believing what he'd heard. And then a slow grin had spread across his lips. Much to her chagrin, Kristen had returned it.

Now, though, in his apartment, the cheer faded from his face, his brow furrowing.

She couldn't look at him, knew what he was going to ask and answered before he could. "Three months is a long time to keep a secret from Gabriel. I didn't want him to know."

"That's what bothered you." Luke sighed. "Gabriel knowing you chose *me*."

She closed her eyes, but it only made things worse, memories playing like silent films on the backs of her eyelids. Kristen fluttered her eyes open, casting away her thoughts, but the truth haunted her whether she acknowledged it or not. Always had. In every memory of Luke, of the two of them together, she was smiling.

"I hid it from him." He said it so quietly that she almost didn't hear him. "So he wouldn't see when he went into your mind."

"I know," she said. She didn't ask why, wondering for the first time if maybe he did truly care for her.

His lips parted like he wanted to say more, but she shook her head. "Don't."

They watched each other in silence. Eventually, Kristen stood and made her way back to the window. Snowflakes tumbled past. A moment later, he joined her.

"It's snowing again," she said quietly.

He didn't speak, simply ran his hands down her hair, lifted it off her back and over her shoulder. When she didn't move away, Luke closed the last few inches separating them, his arms encircling her waist. His lips brushed her neck, rose to her ear. "I'm cashing in the favor you owe."

Kristen tensed. "So soon?" she asked shakily. "You're sure you don't want to save it for a special occasion?"

He ignored her. "I want you."

"Wait, want me?" He clearly wasn't after a mere house-guest and it was a line Kristen wouldn't cross, no matter what the payoff or the punishment. "Luke, you can't ask for that."

He turned her to face him as he caught her meaning. "Kristen, I want your favor. Your company," he clarified before his grin grew cocky. "Though I don't recall you finding my attentions distasteful."

She raised an eyebrow, trying to look fierce, knowing she wasn't pulling it off. He could have asked for anything, and he'd only asked for time with her?

"For how long?" she asked carefully, trying to think of any other loopholes he could exploit.

He winked at her catch. "One week, clever girl. You'll stay here with me."

She laughed. "You want to play house? You can't be serious."

"I'm offering you a life of freedom. No more bouts of delirium. Every wish granted." Luke smiled. "You give me a week to show you how things can be. At the end of it, you'll choose to stay."

"One week." Kristen licked her lips, let the thought of the life he offered simmer for a moment. "Done," she said, holding out her hand. He shook it. She didn't trust his smile. "So when do we start?"

"We already have," Luke answered.

CHAPTER 20

$\mathcal{A}$z pulled a single key out of the pocket of his coat by the tattered shoelace he used as a lanyard. Jarrod followed him into the apartment building, Sullivan beside him. It was a good distance from home, far enough to be discreet but close enough that if Eden called, Jarrod could get there by cab within ten minutes. He practically sighed in relief when Az headed them down the stairs. No balconies. Sullivan seemed serious about wanting to quit, but he didn't know if it would be like other drugs. Withdrawal. It might get ugly. One less worry after last night.

Az paused at the door. "Fair warning, we left in a hurry. Might be a bit messy." He shrugged. "Beggars can't be choosers, right?"

He opened the door as he said it, but none of them were prepared for the sight. The apartment was trashed. A smashed television was overturned in the center of the living room, the couch slit alongside the back, material dangling loose in a wide arc.

"Messy's a bit of an understatement, man." Jarrod moved aside to let Az pass.

The apartment was frigid.

"Looks like this is how they got in," Sullivan said, heading to the open window, sliding it shut. "Well, at least now we know we'll be earning our keep cleaning up the place."

"This sucks," Az whispered, squatting down to survey the totaled television.

"Gabriel?"

Everyone froze. The voice came from down the hallway.

Sullivan stood by the window, the cord to the blinds wrapped around her hand. Jarrod didn't know whether to cross the room to her or stay where he was. Az didn't look at him. He'd crouched a bit, his hands out and ready to fight.

"Who is it?" Jarrod whispered. Az gave his head a slight shake, his forehead furrowed.

Jarrod shifted enough to get a look down the hallway. One of the doors was open. A shadow fell over the white carpet, cast from the light spilling out of the room.

"Who comes?" the voice called. The words sounded slightly off, as though translated from another language. Something was wrong with the actual voice, too; the slightest echo of metal against metal ended each word.

Jarrod turned to Az, confused.

Az's eyes blazed red. Not the subtle rusty color Jarrod had seen in them when Eden pissed him off, but freaky-ass, horror-movie demon red.

"Jesus Christ," Jarrod whispered.

From behind them, Sullivan asked, "What? Who is it?"

She couldn't see Az's face. "Jarrod, take her and get out of here. Go," Az said.

Jarrod opened his mouth to protest, but the shadow had already started down the hallway.

His movements weren't quite steps, his legs lifting like they were pulled by puppet strings, like he'd never walked before.

Az turned to Jarrod. The red was gone from his eyes. They'd shifted to almost orange as the rusty anger mixed with the yellow color of fears. "Don't let me go *anywhere* with him," Az said desperately. "No matter what I say."

"Who is it?"

"Michael," Az whispered. "Bound. The one from the other night."

As the figure moved closer, Jarrod could see the face had angel written all over it, that carved-marble look too perfect to belong to a real person. The same dark curly hair as Az. He could have passed for his brother.

"Arrogant enough to ignore a summons, Az? How

dare you be so defiant?" Michael stopped a few feet in front of Az.

"Be easy," Az said, his voice strange, copying that same weird diction. "I have no allegiance. I've made it clear I have no interest in such. You shouldn't be here."

"I run this realm when the end times come to the mortals. The end times come with the Pathless ones."

"What, so the Siders are ending the world?" Jarrod said, and regretted it instantly. Michael's attention shifted to him and revulsion overtook his face.

"Don't even think about it, Michael." Az jumped in front, shoving Jarrod back. He had a hand on Michael's chest.

"I can bring you back to glory before we burn this world," Michael whispered.

"You can't kill the Siders."

"We learn." Michael laughed, a wicked, dead drone. "Even now we watch one."

Az's jaw clenched. "Stay the fuck away from Eden."

Michael edged closer. "The first strains of death claim your whore."

Az tipped forward, fists gripped tight at his sides. Jarrod tensed, expecting him to throw a punch at Michael, but suddenly Az's face paled. "She's *not* dying. She can't."

"Such emotion! Is it because you've witnessed the malady yourself? The truth burns your anger so bright."

The laugh came again, and Jarrod shivered. "You falter. Choose Upstairs, Azazel."

"I *choose* to stay *here*." Az's voice was hard. Jarrod kept his eyes on him, didn't want to look at the other one.

"Use the wings!" Michael spat, drawing closer to Az.

"Never!" Az bellowed. Crackling sparks shot between his lips.

A low electrical hiss drifted out of him.

Jarrod knew the sound. It was the same noise he'd heard at the apartment when Az's eyes went all white, right before the chittering started. Az opened his mouth, eyes rolled up a quarter of the way. They didn't look right, like he was possessed.

Michael's eyes had blanked out like hard-boiled eggs, light shining from inside them until they glowed, the shine seeping from his nostrils, flickering across the curls hanging over his ears. Az jerked as if he tried to pull away and couldn't. A bulge ran down his back, fabric ripping. *The wings,* Jarrod thought.

"No!" Jarrod yelled. "He's not yours!" He leaped, knocking Az over. A jolt of electricity shot up Jarrod's arm, slammed the air from his lungs.

Az broke the trance and pushed Jarrod away. "Door. Run. Go!"

Each word came out more desperate than the last. Jarrod ran straight into Sullivan and the three of them barreled out the door, yanking it closed behind them. Az tripped and plowed shoulder first into threadbare carpet covering the concrete floor of the building's entrance. He rolled up to a sitting position with a hiss, holding his arm as he struggled to his feet.

Sullivan's eyes were unfocused. Jarrod stood in front of her, but her gaze went right through him. He thought of the story of her reaction to Vaughn telling her about being a Sider. *Completely catatonic,* she'd said.

"Move," Az demanded. He didn't even bother talking to her, grabbed one of her hands and threw her over his hurt shoulder. "We gotta go."

Az carried Sullivan down the street, took a side street and then another, twisting their route until they were only a few blocks away from home. "Call Eden. Tell her to meet us, door open." He hoisted Sullivan's deadweight, groaning as he adjusted her.

Jarrod took out his phone but didn't put the call through. "Az, is something wrong with Eden?"

He spun to Jarrod. "Of course not. He was bluffing, trying to mess with my head. But look," he said, his eyes downcast. "When we tell her what happened, we're gonna leave that whole last part out, okay? She worries enough anyway."

Jarrod didn't look at him, kept walking. "Eden and I don't do secrets."

"And normally no secrets is great," Az said, licking his lips. "But it's not going to do her any good to be worrying about some stupid lies of Michael's. Right?" He grabbed Jarrod's arm, pulled him to a stop. "Right, Jarrod?" Az said again.

Sullivan gave a soft sob. Jarrod brushed her hair back from her clammy skin. Her lips moved in repetitive motions, eyes wide and unblinking. Jarrod leaned closer to hear. It took him a second to make out her whispers: "He was on fire inside his head. Inside his head. I saw God. I saw God in his eyes."

Her lips were still going, but her voice faded away. Jarrod cast a glance behind them, but there was no sign of Michael.

"You should call Eden. Sullivan's not doing good, Jarrod. And I wouldn't get Eden all upset if you're planning on showing up with her like this."

"Right," Jarrod whispered as he hit Send. Right before the call connected, it hit him. Why Az looked so worried. "Michael was just lying anyway."

"Exactly," Az said, his voice full of relief. He hoisted Sullivan against him.

Lying. Except lying wasn't something the Bound could do.

CHAPTER 21

Behind Eden, in her bed, Sullivan lay flat. Her breaths had evened out from the erratic gasps she was making when Jarrod had first brought her in, but she wasn't responding much. Eden could hear Jarrod's murmurs to her, though they were too low for her to make out the actual words.

Eden stared out the window of her bedroom. The gloomy storm clouds had finally ditched their haul, tossing down fat, wet flakes for the past hour or so. She'd been watching them get slammed against the red brick of the building beside theirs, caught up in the draft.

Her breath steamed an oval, and she drew a sharp lightning bolt through the center. *Michael.* He'd been there at the apartment, terrifying enough that he'd fried Sullivan's brain something fierce. *But Jarrod is okay. Az is safe.* She smeared away the fog on the window. *Lucky,* she thought. *Incredibly lucky.*

Mostly.

Twice Sullivan had called out and then faded back into that zombified state. Each time left Jarrod looking broken and sick.

She turned from the window. Jarrod stared down at Sullivan, the seconds ticking by, wasted. And then an idea broke across his face. Eden saw it, knew he'd thought of something but was second-guessing it.

"Whatever it is, you should try it. She's not getting any better."

He flicked his eyes to Eden and away, as if embarrassed.

She thought for sure he'd shake the girl, rattle her brains back into place. Instead, he ground one of his shoes against the other and slipped out of it, did the same with the second one. He folded the covers all the way down.

Sullivan balled up the second the air hit her. Jarrod didn't hesitate, climbed onto the bed, over her. Eden couldn't be sure, but she thought she saw the girl relax a bit.

"What're you doing?" Eden asked, but he ignored her, closed his eyes.

"Sullivan, it's Jarrod." He scooted even closer and curled up against her back. "You've gotta snap out of this, okay? We've got…" He hesitated as if remembering Eden was in the room. His voice lowered. "It's snowing. You should see how beautiful it is. You should open your eyes."

For a long moment nothing happened, and then

Sullivan uncurled a hand and reached behind her to find Jarrod's gloved fingers. "His eyes were glowing," she said softly.

Jarrod nodded against her shoulder.

"What was he?"

"An angel," Jarrod answered. "The real kind."

Eden took a silent step back toward the window, not wanting to startle her, letting them talk. She wondered how far Jarrod would push it, how much he would tell. Sullivan's shoulders tensed up, but Jarrod's hands were there a second later, massaging.

Eden waited to hear Sullivan argue it, but she didn't, seemed to accept it as Eden watched, fascinated.

"Are you an angel, too?" Sullivan asked. "Is that what the Siders are?"

"No."

Eden looked up at the sound of the door opening.

Az surveyed the scene from the threshold and crossed the room to Sullivan. "Hey! Back with us?"

Sullivan gave him a small smile. "Thank you for carrying me."

She sat up and slid off the edge of the bed. Az offered a hand to help her up. "Think nothing of it."

Suddenly she froze, her hand in his, held above her head. Her grin disintegrated. "You have no gloves. No gloves."

"Shit," Jarrod yelled even before he jumped off the bed. Az yanked away, giving her space.

Sullivan backed into the corner like a frightened animal. "Touching me. They were always touching me. Too much." She wiped her hands on her jeans, sinking to the floor. Jarrod dropped beside her and grabbed her at the wrists with gloved hands.

"Sullivan, no. Look at me, okay?" She listened, focusing on him, but the low murmur of her words didn't stop. "Hey!" he yelled.

She froze.

"Az can't pass you Touch."

"What?" she whispered.

"He can't pass you Touch. He's not like me and Eden."

She sucked in a breath, drew up her knees as she looked at Az. "You're like the glowing one, aren't you?"

"Not entirely," Az managed. He held out his hands as if it would be some reassurance.

Jarrod turned her head toward him. "You trust me, right?" She nodded. "I promise you Az won't hurt you. He's a good guy." Jarrod perked up. "He's got wings! Big ones." He turned to Az. "Will you show her?"

"Jarrod!" Eden admonished. She glanced at Az to get his reaction. "Are you sure this is a good idea right now?"

Jarrod glanced at Sullivan, looked back to Az. "Sullivan's almost as good at keeping secrets as I am." Eden couldn't understand the sudden tension between them. "Show her," Jarrod said, a slight command in his tone.

Az pulled his shirt off, crumpled it in a tight ball, and stood there awkwardly. He hated the wings, kept them hidden most of the time, but she thought they were beautiful. He cleared his throat. His eyes were on Sullivan, gauging her reaction as he unwound the ace bandage from his chest. Eden waited, a little thrill of anticipation winding through her. Slowly, the tip of his right wing peeked out. The girl looked up at him in shock and slowly got to her feet.

"I mean, I thought knowing about Siders was messed up, but this is . . ." Sullivan stepped slowly forward, her hand held out. "Can I?"

Az let out an embarrassed laugh. "I guess so?"

And then she was touching them, touching the feathers on Az's wing, the fear gone from her eyes. "That's just crazy!" Sullivan said, turning excitedly to Jarrod.

When their eyes connected her smile widened, though she shied. "It's not going to get me in trouble to say I still like my angels in the snow?"

Az shrugged and shot Eden a bemused look. She didn't return it, watching as Jarrod's lips skipped across Sullivan's neck tentatively, up her jaw, and met her mouth. Jarrod and Sullivan shared a breath, lips pressed together in a way Eden would never feel with Az. If she ever dared, gave in, her kiss would be what drove him to Fall. Her lips would ruin him.

"I'm sorry, I have to go," Eden managed as she pushed past them. She broke out into the hall.

"Is she okay?" she heard Sullivan ask.

Az answered. "Will you guys be all right?"

And she knew he was coming after her. She headed to the kitchen and threw herself into one of the chairs, blinking furiously. *I'm not going to cry,* she promised herself, lips pressed together in a tight frown.

"What's wrong?" Az asked, rounding the corner into the kitchen. His shirt was still off, his abs movie star worthy, and he was gorgeous and special and hers, and before she knew what was happening the first of her tears had already fallen.

"I'm just tired." She couldn't look at him. She laid her forehead on the table so she wouldn't have to.

"That's it?" Az wrapped her up in his arms from behind and the touch of him, the smell of him, his skin against her, made it so much worse. A sob broke out of her.

"He kissed her. He could kiss her all the time if he wants!" she cried, wiping furiously at her face.

"What does it matter who he kisses?" Az asked.

"Because he *can*. He can kiss her. They can sleep in the same bed. She doesn't have to worry about one wrong brush from her mouth while she *sleeps* taking him away."

She struck out, knocking the napkin holder off the table. It clattered into the living room, and she instantly felt childish for her outburst. "Most of the time I'm okay, I can deal with the trade-off. But sometimes I want you so bad it hurts," she whispered.

His mouth found the nape of her neck, his lips soft on her skin, but it wasn't enough.

"Don't."

He didn't listen, unwrapping his arms from her, his kisses growing more desperate as he made his way down to her shoulder, across it. She gasped as he yanked her chair around to face him, slid himself on top of her lap, straddling her.

"Az, we can't."

He cupped his hand across the back of her head, his eyes solemn. He pulled her closer, kissed a slow line down her temple. Her breath caught when his tongue flicked across the hollow at the base of her neck. "Of course we can."

She felt him smile against her skin.

"Is it about the danger?" he asked, transforming his voice into a sexy growl. "You're afraid?"

He lifted his head slightly, and for a moment she was afraid. That her lips were too close to be safe.

"Stop it!" She pushed him hard enough that the chair almost tumbled over with the two of them in it. "Get off me."

"Give me a second!" Az untangled himself from her,

climbing off looking abashed. "What the hell, Eden?"

She knocked the chair back as she stood.

"I could kill you. One kiss." She sounded out each word. "Without Gabe, I'll be the reason you Fall. The Bound are *here*. Luke is *here*. How much longer before they find me? Take you away? The danger of it's supposed to *turn me on*? Fuck off, Az."

"Where's this coming from?" He crossed his arms over his chest.

"You keep acting like you're fine without Gabe. I don't know what's worse, that you could abandon him so quickly or that you actually believe you're gonna make it without him. You're lying to me again. You promised you wouldn't." Her shoulders slumped. "Is this what you're like without him?"

She looked up when he didn't say anything. He stood stock-still, then broke and grabbed a glass from the cupboard. He filled it at the faucet and took a long draught. When he'd finished, he dropped his hands to the counter, leaning against it with his head down. "Gabe made his choices long before we ended up on that roof, Eden. They were his to make."

She shook her head. "If I hadn't kissed you that day, Luke wouldn't have taken you, and Gabe wouldn't have Fallen, and everything would be fine. You can't make it without him, Az."

"You really don't get it, do you?" he said gently. He lifted a hand to her cheek. "Gabe can only do so much. I love you, Eden. It's *you* who keeps me here, makes me want to stay. You." Az moved his hands to her shoulders. "Don't you get that? I'm trying to do what's right by everyone, and it's screwing everything up. Madeline was Gabe's secret to keep. That's why I didn't tell you."

She didn't answer.

"I was in a basement for hours before Luke took me up to the roof."

"I don't want to talk about it," Eden broke in, but he didn't stop.

"Every minute hurt worse and this voice in my ear, the whole time it kept whispering how easy it would be to Fall, how the pain would go away. Hour after hour," he said, stroking her shoulder softly with each word. "But I wouldn't listen. Because I knew no matter how much it hurt, it would hurt you more if I gave in."

She sniffled.

"Gabe had nothing to do with me making it through that day, Eden. It was you. It's still you. It's always going to *be* you." Her hand rested against his chest, his heart beating strong under her fingers. "If I made it through that day on the roof, I can make it through anything else. They can pressure me, they can try to sway me, but I'd never choose to leave you. Gabe knew that. He's counting on it."

She traced his breastbone down. "I really wish I could kiss you right now."

"Personally, I think we got the better deal." Fingertips stole under the back of her shirt, followed either side of her spine up. His hands wandered from her shoulders to her chest and then her hips, teasing her closer. "Jarrod can't touch Sullivan."

Eden paused. He was right. She looked down at her hand on Az's chest, the feel of his skin under her bare fingertips. She and Az could have contact all the time, constantly.

He tightened his grip on her, bending back to lift her off her feet, and twirled her in a slow circle. She giggled. It felt silly, laughing in the kitchen with her face all splotchy and tears still drying on her cheeks.

And then Az's smile faded. The fingers that had explored her skin with such need were tentative as he touched her cheek.

"What is it?" she asked, not quite wanting to know, to let go of the moment.

"It's nothing," he said, moving his hand down, but she grabbed it. He wouldn't look at her as she pulled it back up.

The tips of his fingers were flecked black.

CHAPTER 22

Cold night air. Gabe's skin was slick so the chill felt good, almost sinful. In the distance, a drunken laugh rang out. From closer came a choked moan. Gabe's hands cramped.

Fingers clawed at his, weakly.

Sweat coursed off him. Between his fingers, flesh. He squeezed tighter. *A death at my hands.* A dreamy smile drifted over his lips.

"Stop." A hand touched his shoulder. "You need to stop."

He winced. Shook his head. *Can't stop.*

Everything fell away, foggy, and then . . .

Sudden awareness snapped through him. He gasped, yanked away from the boy's neck, and stumbled.

"Oh fuck," Gabe whispered. He watched horrified as the boy swayed, then dropped like a stone. His head hit against the building on the way down.

"Gabe?" He whipped around, panic seizing him. The girl behind him was a stranger. *She interrupted.* A petite little thing. *Needs to be taught a lesson.* He froze at the dark skitters threatening to overwhelm him, the punishments he'd dole out. *She knows your name. She has to die. She knows your name.*

She wasn't a stranger.

"Who are you? Where am I?" He shot a quick glance up. Parking lot. Full. He stood between two cars parked nose first against a brick wall, the boy on the ground in front of him. The girl blocked his escape. He fought the urge to knock her aside and flee.

"My, my, lover!" Her eyes dropped to the curled body at his feet. No, it wasn't a body; the boy was still breathing. Barely. "I let you out of my sight for two minutes." She clucked her tongue, disapprovingly.

Gabe grabbed the hood of a car to steady himself. Everything blurred, the strength running out of his legs. "I'm not your lover."

"Good," she purred. "That's a good start, Gabe. So who am I?"

He lifted his head, shaking it, his eyes squinted in uncertainty. "I don't . . . I don't know." A name clicked across his brain, but it wasn't hers. "Az?" His voice came out high and pleading. "Is Az here?"

She shook her head slowly, her eyes full of pity. "Let's

talk about the Sider, Gabe. What did he say? He made you angry."

He spun, gravel grinding under his boots, staring down at the boy. He opened his mouth to say there was nothing, but then a ghost of a hazy memory drifted to him. "He came here because it's where they always come to sell." He winced. "Touch. He was selling Touch. The mortals. They're getting addicted?" He looked up at her for confirmation.

She nodded approvingly. "More, Gabe. We know those things. You were Downstairs, checking on their paths. Do you remember if you found any of the mortals' paths, Gabe?" A note of desperation crept into her voice, though he knew she didn't want him to hear it. She needed to know what was happening to the mortals who were addicted. Needed him to find out.

"Their paths, they're . . . broken . . . and I couldn't find them sometimes. I couldn't stay long enough." His voice fell to a whisper as he began to remember more. "In and out. You always say in and out. I had to hurry."

The scent of sulfur overwhelmed him. He gagged, dry heaving, and dropped his elbows to his knees. Flashes of memories crowded his head. "Downstairs. The Siders were all in cages." The girl moved closer, put a hand on his back to comfort him. "Don't." He brushed her away. "You shouldn't be so trusting. I'm Fallen, Madeline."

He shot straight. Madeline. She was a Sider. He had known her Before, almost as long as Kristen. When he was different, when everything was so different. A mix of sorrow and terror brought tears to his eyes, everything flooding into him at once.

"Please. Please, I want to go Home." His cry was sudden, ripped through him.

Madeline blinked hard. "When you knew you were going to Fall, that you weren't going to be able to resist much longer, you wrote me a letter. Do you remember? You told me the things you couldn't say out loud."

They were coming to him, fast and clear. He nodded.

"You told me that if you were going to Fall, you wanted to help us figure out what was going on, that I should have you go Downstairs. Spy."

Gabe gasped, her words calling up bits of memory. "Luke tricked the Siders. He has them in cages, and they can't pass Touch. They're going mad! All of them except . . . One. She's sick, though. Something's wrong with her." He shook his head, trying to focus. "She's falling apart." His head snapped up. "Eden. My God, you have to tell Az it's going to happen to Eden!"

"You told me about this, Gabe." Madeline squeezed his hand. "I'm trying to help Eden. I promise."

"It's so hard to concentrate." Gabe felt like he was being ripped in two. Dark thoughts bubbled below his consciousness. Pressure building like a steam valve. "Cold," he whispered.

Madeline skidded back from him, suddenly cautious, digging in her pocket. "Give me just a second," she said as she pulled out a small orange bottle. She uncapped it and shook out the contents. "We're out of time. Here."

She held out her hand, palm up. In the center rested a tiny white tablet. "Put it under your tongue."

"You're drugging me?" His confusion lasted only a second. "You're the one giving me the blackouts?" *She dares cross you?* Rage crackled through him.

He slid closer to her, around her, until *she* was the one cornered against the bricks. *Doesn't she realize what a helpless thing she is?*

"Gabe, take the pill!"

He could smell the sudden fear on her skin, in the air. It fed his need, urged him on. He crept nearer. "You think I'm your puppet? That I'll do your bidding?"

She turned her face from him, wincing as he pressed her against the wall. "Gabe, stop. You had a note that brought you here. I wrote it."

His irritation blazed. He ached for her screams, to feel her struggle against him. She didn't react, held perfectly still. Why wasn't she fighting? He walked his fingers slowly across her throat, the tips sliding over the side of her neck. *Squeeze.*

"And before that, there was a note *you* wrote," she said, her voice quivering. Her pulse jackhammered under his thumb. "It told you to remember what Az said." He felt a twinge of hesitation but ignored it, curled his hand around her neck. "What did Az say?" she screamed.

"'Trust only Madeline.'" The words left his lips instantly.

Gabe froze. A memory lurched to the surface, his hand aching as he scrawled the words over and over, imbedding them in his mind while he was still Bound. He would be too dangerous to be near Az, and Eden would be with Az. Kristen would be devastated, angry. But Madeline could be trusted. She'd gleaned enough experience through Luke to know how to work the Fallen. *Never run when they see you as prey.* Words he'd written in the letter.

He realized his hand was still on Madeline's neck and dropped it, embarrassed.

She shuddered in a relieved breath. "'Trust Madeline.'" She held out her hand again. "And I am Madeline. And I'm telling you to take this. Now." She pinched the tablet between her fingertips, gave it to him. "Under your tongue, Gabe. You have to trust me."

"What is it?"

She shook her head, the color starting to return to her cheeks. "I don't know. But they're from you. They came with the letter. You said you used to be able to catch thoughts when you were Bound. You didn't know if the

Fallen could, too, and we can't let them find out what you're looking for. The pill fades you in and out so you don't remember me. Don't remember being Downstairs. What you've learned."

He stared down at the pill.

"It also helps keep you from being violent, Gabe. Please take it." She swallowed. "You didn't used to want to hurt anyone. Don't you feel that way still? Even a little?"

"No," he managed. But he wanted to. He lifted his tongue, nestled the pill underneath. Bitterness flooded his mouth, and he winced.

"It tastes terrible but dissolves almost instantly." She edged past him, leery, as they walked out from between the cars. "Which means it works fast." He looked back, at the boy he'd been choking. "He's a Sider," she said. "Better that you hurt him than a mortal. He'll heal in a few hours."

"How long have we been doing this? What am I looking for?" he asked, following her.

"Originally you were supposed to gather whatever info you could, but then you started talking about Luke holding the Siders captive. We started hearing about mortals being addicted, so you've been looking into what happens with their paths. I only get pieces from you. It's not ideal, but it's what we have." She pulled her coat tighter around her.

"Madeline . . ."

She held up, trusting him enough to wait for him to catch up and stand beside her.

"How are they? Az? Eden?" Even their names shot a pang through him.

She paused as if debating telling him, and he knew it wouldn't be good. "Az is struggling," she said finally. "I'm worried about him. Especially if you're right about what's happening to Eden."

"What's happening to Eden?" he asked.

She laughed, the sound breaking across the parking lot like shattered glass, though her lips hadn't moved. *No*, he realized. Someone had thrown a bottle. His brain felt numb, confused.

"She's being stubborn." Madeline's voice was strange, echoing and distant.

Everything blurred, dim and unsteady. *Fingers wrapped around bars. Dirty blond hair. Ashes. So many ashes.* He blinked and felt leather against his cheek, a seat. The hum of tires. He moaned and raised his head.

A hand at his waist helped him along. He stumbled up a set of stairs.

"Almost there," Madeline soothed him. "You're home, Gabe."

Blackness.

CHAPTER 23

The leather of the couch creaked under Kristen as she shifted and opened her eyes. She felt strange, alert, and clearheaded. The typical moment of confusion between sleep and consciousness, when she realized she wasn't in her own bed, never came. She knew exactly where she was. Truth be told, she felt better rested than she had in a month. Perhaps because every second was no longer a battle to hold herself together, to pretend she was all right. She stretched, swallowing. Her throat felt raw and dry.

She could see her phone on the coffee table, on silent but the screen aglow with missed messages. Reaching out, she snapped it up as quietly as she could. Her heart sank. Fifteen texts from Sebastian.

"Damn it," she whispered. Her anxiety flared back full force. She held the phone in her hand, her fingers paused above the keys. What to say? My apologies for worrying you. I felt it best to take a few days by myself.

Please attend to everyone as you see fit.

She hit Send, wondering how he'd react. It was the first time she'd done anything like this, taken off and left him in complete control. What if he thought she was in danger, came looking for her? Shame rolled through her.

"I had no choice," she murmured.

"You keep saying that." She startled. Luke stood behind her. "Last night, you were talking in your sleep. Begging for forgiveness." He ran a hand through his curls, rubbed an eye sleepily. "It was rather pathetic, to be honest."

"Almost as pathetic as you creeping close enough to hear me." She threw the blanket off and then paused. When she'd fallen asleep, there'd been nothing over her.

Luke ran a hand on the back of his neck. "You were screaming, Kristen. I barely slept."

"I'm sure I wasn't screaming," she snapped, but the hoarseness of her throat betrayed her. Her voice softened with embarrassment. "Why didn't you wake me?"

Luke strolled into the kitchen. "Now how much sense would it make to shut you up when you were spilling so many lovely secrets?"

Kristen's heart stalled. "Such as?"

He glanced over the island counter and caught sight of her face. "Gibberish, mostly. Apparently you keep your secrets even in your sleep." He grabbed a Tupperware container full of cereal down from the cabinet. "I know you don't have to eat, but would you join me for breakfast?"

She wanted to tell him no, to stride out the door and never see him again. For the first time she wondered if Luke had planned all along to give her the information she needed to find Gabriel. Because after seeing him on the train, the cruelty in his eyes, she knew there was nothing she could do for him. That at least for the time being, Luke was the only one she could turn to.

"That would be fine." Leaning against a wall in the kitchen, she rubbed her arms. She shivered without the warmth of the comforter. "Is it always so cold in here?" she asked.

He glanced around the room, surprised, and then shrugged. "I'm sorry, I didn't realize. I guess it's not cold to me. We can turn up the heat if you'd like, but I doubt it'll do much good."

The wording gave Kristen pause. "Why wouldn't it do any good?"

"It's an older building. The penthouse has a wonderful view of the city, but it's drafty." Luke took two bowls from the cabinet, spoons from a drawer. "I'd say I'm surprised you didn't notice the other times you were here but things were a bit . . . hotter . . . then."

He winked before going back to pouring the cereal into bowls.

"Is that Lucky Charms?" Kristen didn't hide her amusement.

He rolled his eyes. "My one weakness, aside from you."

"Laying it on a bit thick, no?" She grabbed one bowl and poured in milk while shaking her head. "Big, bad Lucifer eating marshmallow cereal. That just makes my morning."

He spooned a mouthful, chewing thoughtfully. "If it really takes so little to make you happy, my surprise will short-circuit you."

Kristen's spoon froze midway to her mouth, her hackles raising. "What do you mean? What surprise?"

Luke looked pleased with himself as he dug into the bowl again. "It's in my room."

"Do girls fall for that?" Kristen asked, unamused.

He met her eyes with a knowing grin that made her despise herself for asking. "You did once," he reminded her. He laughed when she huffed. "Oh, relax. I said it's in the room, not under the covers."

She abandoned her bowl on the counter. Halfway down the hall, she glanced back at Luke, but he only shooed her forward. The door was open, the room beyond it immaculately clean. Luke kept the room stripped of everything but the essentials, and looking like it'd been taken directly from an edgy decorating magazine. Maroon walls, white accents, the bed with its elegantly spindled headboard and black sheets. She didn't want to think of the other girls he'd no doubt brought there.

"I don't see anything," Kristen said.

She walked all the way into the room. Her reflection stared back at her from the mirrored double doors of the closet. The wild eyes that always greeted her in the mirror at home were not the ones looking back at her from Luke's mirrors. These eyes were focused and a bit amused. The smile faded from Kristen's face and the reflection stared back, solemn. Her dress was wrinkled, but for being slept in, wasn't bad. Her hair was still the typical unruly mess.

"'While the sad wind goes slaughtering butterflies,'" Kristen murmured to herself. She finger combed it into submission.

"'My happiness,'" Luke said from behind her, coming closer, "'bites the plum of your mouth.'"

Kristen raised an eyebrow. "You know Neruda?"

Instead of answering, he let his fingers slip across her collarbones, through the shallow cleft between them, down, lingering. Luke met her eyes in the mirror. "'I want to do with you what spring does with the cherry trees.'"

She groaned as a blush broke across her face. "What, pollinate them?"

"No," Luke said, and tripped the switch that slid the mirror to the side and opened the walk-in closet. "Drape them in beauty."

Her breath caught. Gowns, sundresses, cocktail dresses, velvets and lace, some flowing, some tight, every color of the rainbow. She ran her fingers over dress after dress, astounded. With effort, she forced the wonder from her voice. "You think I can be bought with pretty things?"

Luke chuffed in disbelief before she turned her attention back to the dresses. "You're a black hole of a girl, Kristen," he snapped.

"And to think," she said. "Most guys would have kept on with the poetry."

"Most guys aren't worthy of you. I am. And you are worthy of me. You see my gifts for what they are. You're a challenge." He twisted her to face him. "I won't insult you with bribery again."

Her exasperated sigh brimmed with enough sarcasm to be sure he caught it. "I'm keeping the dresses," she said, and a laugh burst out of him.

One of his hands slid from her shoulder, down her waist to her hip. He curled it around her back and dipped her as if they were slow dancing. She fell back, trusting his strong grip to hold her without thinking. When he tightened his arm to bring her up again, she found herself pressed against him, staring into his eyes.

His tongue slid slowly across his lips. "My little black hole," he said, leaning his head nearer to her. "Pulling me in."

CHAPTER 24

$\mathcal{E}$den bolted up, a scream halfway up her throat before she cut it off. Someone grabbed her hand. She yanked away, couldn't see anything in the dark, frantically fumbling on the nightstand trying to find the lamp.

"Hey, it's okay! It's me!" Az said as she clicked on the light. He yanked her thick drapes open, letting in the morning light.

She sucked air in, trying to catch her breath, get her bearings. Having Az beside her was enough to slow her heart, take the edge off her panic.

"Holy shit," she whispered. She closed her eyes and fell back, raising the covers up and curling into a ball.

"Nightmare?" he asked. She didn't answer. "It sounded like a bad one. I heard you from the couch."

He dropped his hand onto her shoulder. The blanket shifted as she unwrapped herself, reaching behind her for his hand. "Don't leave, okay? Please?"

She pulled his arm around her. His fingers twisted around hers as he curled close.

"What was it about?" he asked. She pulled his hand to her stomach.

"I thought it was snowing." She tried to lick her lips, but her tongue still felt dry and gritty, like it'd been in the dream. "We were on the roof again and . . . I thought it was snowing, but it was ashes. Everywhere. And then they had you." Her breath hitched, and she felt his lips press against her shoulder. "The Fallen. The Bound. Both of them. They were fighting over you." She squeezed his hand. *He's here,* she thought. *He's okay.* The unease clung to her anyway. "And you were . . . God, I don't think I'll ever get the sound out of my head." She couldn't say it.

"What sound, Eden?"

She fought to keep the tears from spilling over. "The way you screamed when they ripped you apart. And I tried to scream, too, but nothing came out. Only ashes."

Goose bumps raised on his arm and she felt guilty for telling him at all. He said her name softly, the tone full of trepidation.

"It was a stupid dream. Probably because of the packages." There'd been another at their door yesterday. She'd thrown it away without opening it.

"When are you going to tell me what's really going on?"

She stiffened. "I don't know what you're—"

Az jerked his arm away from her. "Stop fucking around, Eden." He dropped back onto the pillows. "Quit pretending we're both oblivious and talk to me about this."

She startled at his anger. He'd clearly been bottling it up. *For how long?* she wondered. She'd tried so hard to hide everything, to not worry him. "Az, I—"

"Are you sick?" he cut in, frustration in his voice. She heard the click of his throat as he swallowed. "Or is it worse?"

She opened her mouth to set him at ease, but no sound would come.

"I didn't think you could get sick," he said quietly. Az was worried, and for the first time she admitted to herself how terrified she'd become.

Something was very, very wrong.

On the nightstand her cell phone alarm went off. For a long moment neither of them moved to shut it off.

"You don't sleep. Sometimes you seem like you're hurt." Finally, Az handed her the phone to silence. "What's going on?"

She gave him the only answer she could. "I don't know. I don't know what's happening to me."

He hadn't mentioned the smears on her cheeks, her hands. She didn't want to admit to herself what they were.

She lifted an arm over her head, adjusting on the pillows so she could see him better. "It could be anything,

Az. I'm not like the other Siders, because of Gabe. For all I know, a few cramps are normal when I stop carrying so much Touch. You weren't around after the rave, but I didn't feel right until I'd balanced out."

She tried to smile.

He moved slowly closer, lying beside her on the pillow. She faced him, didn't dare shy away from the intensity in his stare, his desire to believe her. *This isn't lying,* she promised herself. *I don't know* what *the pain means, let alone the ashes.*

Az kissed the top of her head. "You're gonna be late," he said as he rolled over.

She rubbed her hands over her face, and then stretched. "Ugh, I can't deal with Madeline this early in the morning."

"Couldn't you have asked her about Sullivan over the phone?"

"There are other things we need to talk about." Eden climbed out of the bed and dressed quickly. "Like Vaughn. But speaking of Sullivan," she said, "Jarrod was worried about leaving her alone. Go easy on him for me, okay?"

Az rolled onto his back and threw his hands behind his head. "He thinks I'm going off the deep end every five seconds."

"Well," she said carefully, "how would you feel if it was him in danger of Falling instead of you? You'd want me to be cautious around him, right?" She slipped into the coat hanging on the handle of her closet door.

Az grumbled as he snuggled deeper into the pillows.

Eden almost let it go, but turned back at the threshold. "Jarrod's gotten both of us out of trouble. The *least* you can do is go easy on him."

She grabbed her keys and left the apartment. She didn't hesitate when she hit the security door, hoping if she hurried that she could be mostly past before the Siders started in on her. The second she was out, though, she screwed up. She let a boy of about sixteen make eye contact.

"I'm not doing that anymore," she said before she thought better of it.

"Yeah," one boy snipped back. "We kind of figured that out. Thanks for the heads-up, though."

Eden paused. "Okay, so what are you doing here?"

The boy hopped down off the railing, strolling across the stone stair, toward her. "Oh, well, look who's interested!"

"What do you want?" she demanded.

"Not you." The boy's smile sent a chill down her back.

"Fuck it," she said, trying to keep the waver from her voice. "Stay if you want. I don't have time for this." She'd taken another two steps when she spun suddenly. "Are you dealing Touch on my stairs?" she accused. The Siders glanced at one another, a few casting down their eyes.

He snorted a laugh. "Thought you didn't have time for this?" Eden waited. "You wanna stop me?" he said, spreading his hands low and far apart. "Stop me."

Eden slowly descended the rest of the stairs, staring back over her shoulder. The boy didn't look away.

As Eden walked into Milton's, the bell on the door jangled. She kicked the snow from her boots, moved to take her gloves off and thought better of it.

After she'd bought her coffee, she sat watching the door.

Madeline nearly skipped to her table a few minutes later.

"So," Madeline started, dropping into her seat. She unwrapped the cupcake she'd purchased on the way in with a flourish of dainty tugs and cut into it with her fork. "Ready to take care of my little Vaughn-shaped problem?"

"You didn't find Jarrod. That was the deal, wasn't it?"

"One of them. You've made several. I'm the only one who seems to be coming through for you." Madeline stared at her for a long second. "How's Az?"

"Not so good," Eden said quietly.

"If there is a way to find Gabriel, Luke'll know it, but it'll be a hell of a challenge getting it out of him. I don't want to push him too much and make him suspicious." She took a forkful of chocolate frosting, smashed the tines down on a few wayward crumbs. "Have you tried to get hold of Kristen?" Eden didn't miss the flash in her eyes before she dropped them, knew Madeline just well enough to sense the uncertainty in her.

"I haven't." If Luke realized Madeline played both sides, he'd torture her slowly, probably give her time to heal and then start over again. What if he thought Kristen was doing the same thing? "You?"

Madeline shook her head. "I'm worried she's had a breakdown." She glanced up when Eden didn't say anything. "You know she's schizophrenic?"

Eden took a quick drink. "I didn't officially. I mean, I knew she was off, but I thought . . . Well, I thought it was Kristen."

Madeline folded the cupcake wrapper, halving it absently. "Gabe helped her. I don't know how. But he slipped up once and said something about—" She stared at the ceiling, trying to recall the exact wording. "'Untangling Kristen.'"

Not only did I take Gabe from Az, but I took him from Kristen, too. Eden dropped her head to her hands and took a breath. "So, what do we do? How do we find her? I'll help you."

"Yeah, you've done a great job proving how reliable you are, Eden." Madeline wouldn't look at her. "Kristen's schizophrenia gets worse without Gabe. And now Kristen's missing. Luke's missing."

Eden took a swallow of hot coffee, the liquid burning her throat. "You're not saying she went to Luke for help? You're mistaken," Eden said carefully. "She wouldn't turn to him. A month ago she gave me the Touch that helped us beat Luke!"

Madeline shrugged. "All I'm saying is that you should watch your back a bit more. Just in case."

"Well, aren't you helpful?" Eden stared her down. "So, why not help me again? Vaughn sold Touch like a drug. The mortals he sold to, what happens if they keep getting hit with Touch? Are they getting addicted?"

A flicker of surprise crossed Madeline's face, almost too fast to catch, but Eden had caught her off guard. She smiled. Madeline did not.

"Some of them got it too often, didn't they?" Eden pressed.

"Now where'd you get an idea like that?" Madeline asked. She laid the fork down on her plate.

"Kristen was always so adamant that Touch be spread out. You knew they'd get hooked, didn't you? You all did." Eden sipped her coffee, trying not to sound accusing and confrontational. Madeline wasn't the enemy. "It worked out great for Vaughn. If he was selling Touch, he had to have them coming back for more, right?"

Across from Eden, Madeline straightened. "That's a very specific theory, Eden." She shoved a bite of cupcake in her mouth, swallowed it, and tapped the napkin lightly against her lips. "Tell me why you really wanted to know and I'll spill it."

"A girl showed up here, at Milton's. Jarrod was with her in her hotel room. She tricked him into touching her."

"Yeah, ton of trickery in that," Madeline snickered. Eden ignored her.

"This girl claims she was with Vaughn. Now, you're well aware of how trusting I am." Eden's smirk was bitter. "I want to know if you can confirm her story."

"Why?" A moment later her expression shifted to amusement. "I mean, I know you have a thing for taking in strays, but mortals?"

"What can I say," Eden deadpanned. "I'm a giver."

Madeline's attention shifted over Eden's shoulder. She froze for a split second, then snapped back to Eden. "Are you seriously trying to pull this on me?" she hissed. "After all I've done for you?"

A shocked laugh burst out of Eden. She bit the inside of her cheek to stifle it when she realized Madeline wasn't kidding. "Pull what? I don't under-stand, Madeline."

"Now you're just pissing me off." Madeline slid out of the booth.

"Wait! What's wrong?" Eden asked. She followed Madeline up.

Madeline spun back to her, rage narrowing her eyes. Eden stumbled backward, but Madeline grabbed her arm, yanked her along to the front door. "Tell me, Eden, what'd Vaughn promise you? You take care of me and he'll make all your problems go away? Did he tell you where Gabe is?" She stopped suddenly, registering the shock on Eden's face. "Jesus Christ, you have no idea we're being watched, do you?"

"Watched?" Eden looked behind her, but Madeline pulled her away out the door and around the side of the building.

"Swear to me you've never seen him before." She pointed through the window at a booth two behind where they'd been. A guy sat there, one leg on the bench, bent with a magazine balanced on it, his head inclined away from them enough to keep his face hidden. He flipped the page, looking completely engrossed. At first all she could see was his gelled-back black hair, but then there was a crash near the counter and he looked up for a split second.

"I've never seen him before," Eden said without hesitation.

Madeline grabbed her by the wrist, marched her back through the door. "Follow my lead. Try to look like a scary bitch," Madeline said over her shoulder. At the booth, she kicked her tennis shoe up on the bench and leaned forward onto her knee. Madeline's hands flew up in mock surprise before she lowered her head into her palms. "Fancy meeting you here, Ali!"

The guy slapped the magazine down on the table. "Pretty far from Queens, Madeline!" He gasped. "Did you get lost?" The smile fell from his face. "Fuck off. I'm not here for you. I'm passing through." He turned to Eden, stared at her for a second. "Who's she?"

Now it was Madeline's turn to balk. "Ali, seriously, I can't take your shit right now. Drop the act."

He shook his head slowly. "No clue, Maddy. Do I need one?"

Madeline let out a squeak of a laugh, looking from Eden to the guy. "Oh, this is too much." She lowered her voice. "You don't know Eden?"

His face went ashen. "That's the death breather?"

"Fifty bucks is usually the going rate for my services." Eden tilted her head, let a smile play at her lips. "But I can always make an exception," she said sweetly. *That ought to cover being a scary bitch,* Eden thought.

He held up his hands. "I said I'm not here for trouble."

"Actually," Madeline cut in, "you said you weren't here for me. So why are you here?"

He ran a hand across the rough stubble on his jaw. He dropped his foot onto the floor, pointed to the bench beside him. They slid in. "There was a girl staying with us. Mortal. All Vaughn wants is the girl back. No trouble."

"So she took off on you?" Madeline asked. "Vaughn doesn't take in mortals. What's the deal?"

"Mortal or not, Sullivan's one of us. Vaughn takes care of his own." Ali relaxed a bit. "Before he had everything set up, we didn't have enough buyers. Vaughn didn't want us spreading to the general public. Luckily, Sullivan was game for a finger tapping whenever we felt the need."

Eden's rage bubbled up at his smarmy smile. "You're sick," she spat. Only a subtle bump of Madeline's elbow into her side kept her from losing it completely. A steady ache blossomed around where she'd been hit, much more hurt than she should have felt from the jab. Eden gripped the edge of the table, preparing herself for the worst.

Ali looked to Madeline as if she'd protect him. "Look, I'm the first to say she's been dosed too many times. I mean, she's spent days so knuckled out she didn't even know where she was half the time, but she has everything she could want. We take good care of her. She's a little confused."

"Why would you think she's in Manhattan?" Madeline crossed her arms on the table. "Counting on her wandering into the coffee shop you're hanging out in doesn't seem like the best plan."

Ali laughed and glanced out the window. "I'm waiting on Vaughn. He got a tip that she was around here. Heard there was a kid who could tell him where to find her. He works here. Vaughn figured he'd try to catch him before he made it."

"Where's Vaughn right now, Ali?" Madeline demanded.

The smile waned as Ali picked up on Eden's growing stress and realized his obvious mistake. "He's part of your crew. You're the one hiding Sullivan."

Eden took off, out through the door. It was after ten. Jarrod would already be on his way to work. Should have been there already.

A car horn blared, the bumper almost swiping her leg as she darted across the street, running full tilt for the alley, already knowing she would be too late.

CHAPTER 25

Jarrod groaned at the screaming alarm, shooting his hand to the floor. He felt around till he found his cell phone, checked the time, and hit the snooze button again. He should have been out of bed and ready by now. Sullivan's arms tangled around his neck.

"Why are we waking up?" she rasped.

"I have to work." He rolled closer to her, drew her against him. Her skin was hot against his, feverish. He dropped his cheek to her forehead. She was burning up. "You feel okay?"

She shrugged. "I just woke up. I don't feel anything but tired." Her eyes still closed, she laid her head on his chest, sighing contentedly. "You make a good pillow."

"Yeah, well, you're gonna have to settle for this one," he said, sliding out from underneath her and replacing himself with the pillow he'd been using.

"How long are you going to be gone?" she murmured.

"It's a full shift, so eight hours." Part of him wanted to bring her with him. She could hang out and he'd know she was safe, but he knew he was being stupid. Vaughn could find her more easily at Milton's. Anyone could. She'd be safer here. And if she was sick . . .

Her face was pale except for two bright burning spots of red on her cheeks.

She's mortal. She's going to get sick. I can't call off for that. If he got fired, they'd never make rent, and they were way too close anyway. He'd already cut out early once and was damn lucky his day off coincided with meeting her.

"Are you sure you're feeling okay?" She didn't answer. Could it be withdrawal? "Sullivan?" He leaned closer, pushing her hair back. "I gotta be there in a few minutes," he said, but she was out again.

She'll be fine, he promised himself, grabbing a work shirt from his closet and tossing it on over his T-shirt. He yanked on the least wrinkled pair of khakis he could find.

Slipping out, he closed the door as quietly as he could and headed to the front door. Az sat on the couch, the television playing softly.

"Hey," Jarrod whispered.

Az lifted a hand in response.

"Where's Eden?"

"Not here yet." He turned to Jarrod, his face blank.

"Nothing's gonna happen in the few minutes until she gets back to set me off."

Jarrod shrugged into his coat. "I wouldn't be leaving if I thought you were gonna lose it."

Az said nothing.

"Sullivan's . . . I don't know if she's detoxing or what, but she's got a hell of a fever. Check on her later if she doesn't come out?" he asked. "I think Eden freaks her out." He slipped on his shoes, tied a quick double knot.

Jarrod raised his hand to the trim on the door, hesitating. He'd been up last night after Sullivan fell asleep, thinking about what Michael had said—how Eden smelled like fire. That Az had seen something. That he was lying. Az and Eden not talking was what had gotten them into the whole mess. If Az wasn't going to tell her, Jarrod knew he'd have to. Not something he looked forward to.

When Az didn't say any more, Jarrod added, "Let me know if she gets any worse." He headed out before Az answered.

Through the window, he took a quick look around and opened the door to the street. No Siders on the stairs, but the packed-down splotches of snow gave away where they'd been. Otherwise, the cement was covered in four inches of snow.

"Damn it." Jarrod stared down the alley. Drifts rose several feet up against one wall.

He stuck to the other side, where the snow left barely a trace, trying not to get his shoes too wet. Today would suck enough without his feet freezing the whole time.

He yanked his hood down, tried to follow the footprints Eden had left on her way to Milton's to meet Madeline. The wind whipped by bitterly cold, spitting snow, as he trudged forward. His foot caught a patch of ice. He tried to make a grab for the wall, clawing for enough of a grip to stay upright, but ended up on his ass anyway.

"Unbelievable!" he yelled, his tailbone screaming.

A shadow darkened across him. "If I'd known you were my competition, I could've waited for Sullivan to wander back on her own."

Jarrod knocked his hood back as he raised his head to whoever was above him. The guy could have passed for a *Sopranos* bit player, built wide like a jock, slicked-back black hair. *Douche bag,* Jarrod decided. The guy didn't offer him a hand up. "That makes you Vaughn," Jarrod guessed. "You got some balls showing up in Manhattan, man."

Vaughn snorted a laugh. "Yeah, you're a real hard-ass." He leaned against the brick wall on one broad shoulder, looking amused. "See, I can tell by the way you're sitting in the snow there."

Jarrod got to his feet, not giving Vaughn the satisfaction of looking away. *Don't slip. Please don't fall,* he begged. A victory grin curled up the corner of his mouth when he made it without so much as a stumble. "Eden know you're trespassing? You know how she deals with people she doesn't like?"

Vaughn's smirk faded.

"I'm just here for a few words." He spread his hands wide with a smile. "Where is Sullivan? Did you leave her alone?" Jarrod didn't react. "Because if there's anything sharp in the room, she's probably bleeding out." Vaughn's cheek twitched, his expression unreadable. "Anything she can get tied around her neck?" he went on, his hand in a fist at the side of his throat yanking at an imaginary noose.

"I don't know what you're talking about," Jarrod said.

"Or did she start you off slow and go for a roof?" Vaughn went on. "You feel like a hero?" His face went hard. "How're you gonna feel when you have to shove your finger down her throat because she swallowed a couple bottles of pills?" He held up his hand, his finger hooked.

Jarrod didn't say anything for half a minute, the silence broken only by the steady plop of drips from above like a metronome.

"Yeah, I thought so," Vaughn sneered.

Jarrod moved to duck around him, but Vaughn didn't budge. "Maybe you shouldn't have given her Touch in the first place."

Something changed on Vaughn's face. Dropping his attention to the snow, he pressed his boot into the edge of the drift, trampling it down. "What's your name?" he asked.

"Jarrod."

Vaughn nodded as if deep in thought, his eyes still downcast. "Listen, Jarrod, I'm done here. I want my girl back."

"She's not your girl," Jarrod ground out.

"She is." Vaughn's head snapped up. "You've known her a week. Sullivan's been mine since we were both *fourteen*," he roared. "You wanna know pain, Jarrod? Watch your girl smiling the day after you die. Walk up to her on the street. Have her look at you like you're a stranger."

Shock broke Jarrod's anger. "You knew her before you were a Sider?"

"We were together three years before I went Sider. I thought she was cheating on me; turns out she was forgetting all about me." Vaughn winced. "I stayed away. I tried. For a year, and then I ran into her at a club. She didn't even look at me." He tipped his head back, staring up into the rush of snowflakes. "One of my crew hit her friends with Touch the weekend before. She was looking for it. And I thought maybe . . . maybe we could start over." He sighed. "I never should have given it to her."

Jarrod's voice came out a whisper, not the calm demand he'd been shooting for. "She's done with you." He looked toward the end of the alley. He knew he wouldn't be able to go to work now. Not after what Vaughn had said. *Was* there anything sharp in his room? She'd been sleeping when he'd left. What if she woke up? He took a few steps back toward the apartment.

"Listen, you little shit," Vaughn started.

Jarrod turned back as Vaughn's fist cracked into his nose. He dropped to his knees, hands cupped over his face for a split second before he dove forward and slammed into Vaughn's legs.

Vaughn caught him on the way down, ending up on top, pounding his knuckles into Jarrod's face again. Jarrod coughed out a spray of blood, fought to turn his head away. Vaughn's knees pinned his arms into the ground, the next punch cracking a bone in Jarrod's cheek.

Wrestling an arm free, he grabbed Vaughn's ear and twisted with everything he had.

"Son of a bitch," Vaughn yelled, rocking enough to the side so that Jarrod could free his other hand and punch into Vaughn's throat. The cry choked off. Jarrod bucked, throwing Vaughn into the wall. Before Vaughn staggered to his feet, Jarrod was already up. He didn't hesitate, palmed Vaughn's face, and slammed his head against the wall.

Vaughn crumpled.

Gasping for breath, Jarrod dropped his elbows to his knees, his nose dripping crimson onto the snow.

"Dick." He straightened and retched, spitting a glop of bloody mucus. Wiping his face with the sleeve of his coat, he cupped a hand under his nose. His face was already swelling; he squinted to see the way back home.

"Jarrod!" A frantic call from the head of the alley. Eden ran toward him.

He slipped as he stepped toward her and went down on one knee. She got to him in time to grab his elbow and keep him from falling flat.

"Jesus Christ," she said, tilting his head up. The taste of the blood that streamed down the back of his throat made him gag. She looked down at the body in the drift beside them as she slung an arm around Jarrod's waist, trying to help him. "Madeline met me, but halfway through she spotted Vaughn's Second. Freaked out thinking I was setting her up and then had us confront him. Someone told him we have Sullivan."

"And where he could find me?" Jarrod's head snapped up. "Little convenient that you were tied up in that conversation while I was getting my ass kicked."

Eden's eyes flashed back to the entrance to the alley closest to Milton's. "No. Not on purpose. I mean, Madeline, she helped me look for you the other night. She wouldn't. . . ." Eden's hands dropped from Jarrod's jacket. "But Ali said someone called Vaughn and tipped him off you'd be here."

Jarrod coughed hard and dropped his hand, a palmful of blood coloring the snow. "You think it was Madeline? She know about Sullivan?"

"She watches us, Jarrod. She could have seen you with her. And she wants Vaughn dead. She could have thought I'd get pissed off enough to do it."

Jarrod paused. "You gonna?"

"It'll send him Downstairs." In the snow, Vaughn didn't stir. Utterly helpless. One breath, and Eden could end him. Jarrod cupped his nose again, pinching it off.

Finally, Eden grabbed for Jarrod's arm. "I can't do it."

He nodded and leaned heavy on Eden's shoulder. As she headed them back toward the apartment, he couldn't help but wonder at the trail of blood he left behind, leading directly to their door.

CHAPTER 26

Luke wrapped his arm around Kristen's. Their shoulders bumped until their steps evened out and they moved down the sidewalk as one. Kristen couldn't seem to shake her paranoia, the feeling they were being watched, followed. They'd never been in public together, never risked being seen. Or rather, she'd never risked it. Not like this. His hands on her felt treasonous.

She snuck a glance at Luke from the corner of her eye. He looked confident, carefree. Himself. Fear swelled in her as they walked, knowing at any moment they could be seen by the wrong eyes.

She wondered what it felt like to not care. To not depend on others for sanity. To be herself, instead of the caricature she'd created, everything amped up to intimidate. Frighten. Turn away.

She caught her reflection in the windows they passed. The dress fit perfectly. The deep brown hugged her curves as if it were made for her. *Is this who I am?* she thought.

Luke leaned in to her ear. "You haven't passed today."

"Oh," she said, realizing he was right. She wondered how much of her nervousness was Touch building.

She held out her hand to him. He snagged a finger of her glove, pulling it off and tucking it into his pocket. She kept her hand low and to the side, fingers searching out rare snatches of bare skin. Kristen kept her eyes ahead, trying to hold in her sigh with each release.

"You don't pick your victims?" he asked, seeming amused. He kissed her cheek before she could pull away. "How wicked."

"No, that's not how it is. I don't want them to be *victims*." *Don't forget who you are,* a voice whispered in the sound of traffic passing. She hadn't given it a thought when she'd touched them. Her voice betrayed her confusion. "I'm normally so careful."

Luke's fingers laced tighter with hers. "I don't judge. No need for guilt."

Her eyes were drawn away, pulled to a figure ahead in the crowd. He didn't seem much older than she was, clean shaven and smiling, but the words coming out of his mouth didn't match the tranquility in his face. He ranted, standing on a box, a sandwich board draped over him.

"What's going on?" she asked Luke.

"Doomsayer." He rolled his eyes.

Kristen picked up a few words of the rant the closer they came. The deepness of the voice drew her in, gravelly and ancient, spouting from the young body.

"And then all shall perish! And the fires shall consume! Lucifer is battering down your door, people. He is wearing you down! Trying to work his way inside you!" Luke let out a laugh. The zealot turned to them, his eyes full of fervor, on Kristen. "You doubt this, but it is the truth!" He turned back to the rest of the crowd, the ones still ignoring him, turning their eyes away.

"Well," Luke said amiably. "He wasn't far off this time." He pulled Kristen suddenly into his arms, staggering them a few steps together. Kristen felt heat rising to her cheeks.

She shrugged him off, embarrassed by her reaction.

"Maybe we should go?" she started, but Luke seemed caught up in the scene the doomsayer made.

"The end times are near!" The man picked up a bell, swinging his arm up and down. The sound grated on her. She moved toward Luke, but the ground seemed to quiver. *Was that an earthquake?* She glanced around. Everyone else seemed unfazed. She raised her head to the doomsayer. Her jaw dropped open.

Around his head was a thick ceramic crown of thorns, chips the size of BB gun pellet holes marring the surface. His face wobbled in and out of focus as she watched.

"No," she whispered. She squeezed her eyes shut, the doomsayer's scream burning into her.

"Fragile minds are easily broken!" She looked up to find he'd zeroed in on her, as if his message was for her alone. Kristen couldn't tear her attention away. *Luke fixed me. I'm not seeing this.*

His eyes rose to the heavens as he touched a finger to the crown. Blood ran down his face in sudden rivulets. "God will help those who . . ." His shoulders jerked back, his voice shuddering like a skipping record. "Help those who God will help those who . . . God will help those who help."

She was dimly aware of Luke's hand tightening around hers, his words whispered in her ear. "Downstairs, we just help ourselves."

"To what?" she murmured.

He tilted her back against him. His hands wound around her, coursing across her hips, down her thighs. "To whatever we want."

Kristen's breath caught. She bit her lip, closed her eyes, slowly rocking back into him.

A scream erupted from around them.

Her eyes snapped open, flew upward.

The blood, the crown, the thorns. They were gone. Kristen stared, confused. The man standing on the box was boney and unkempt, a scraggly beard hanging down his chest. The doomsayer stabbed a finger at her. "A scarlet letter for whores!" he bellowed. A gob of thick spit hit her cheek.

Kristen gasped. Luke stepped in front of her, wiping her cheek with his sleeve, his eyes burning maroon.

"Say the word, and I'll end him. He'll never say such things again." His voice shook with barely contained anger, waiting for a signal from her, a nod, a word, anything, to break loose. She pictured it, Luke tearing him limb from limb, the crowd screaming. Part of her wanted it. So badly wanted it.

She swallowed, trying to push the images away and shook her head slowly. "He . . . he changed. He didn't look like that before."

Luke turned his glare on the man.

"There'll be Hell to pay for that when the time comes. Rest assured." He grabbed her arm. "Come on," he snarled.

The doomsayer's eyes never left Kristen as Luke dragged her off though the crowd. She stumbled along, certain if she looked away the man would shift and she'd miss it.

When she couldn't see the doomsayer anymore, she finally forced her eyes forward, miserable. Another episode. Hallucinations. *It's starting again.* One morning of sanity, enough time for her to actually believe in the possibility, and already her tenuous hold had slipped away. *What if I can't be fixed anymore?* Kristen's heart sank. She should have known better than to get her hopes up.

Beside her, Luke's fury hadn't dissipated. "The gall of them *astounds* me."

"He couldn't help it. He's not well." She fought for composure, her voice fading to a near whisper. "He's not well like I'm not well," she said quickly. "I thought I was better, that you made me better, but I saw—"

Luke yanked her suddenly to face him. "The crown of thorns? The blood?"

Part of her wanted to weep. "You saw, too? I'm not crazy?"

"They're so dramatic Upstairs," Luke added with disdain, and her relief drained away.

"He was Bound?"

"A lower-ranking messenger. They can only come here when they're called." Luke gripped her arm, stepping them out of the way for the pedestrians streaming past. "What did you do, Kristen?" he sneered. "You say your prayers? Beg them to save you from me?"

He ran his fingers through her hair, a few strands ripping loose when he caught a snarl. She winced. "I was frightened."

"And instead of helping, they only played with you,

exploited your weaknesses." He lifted his hand again, but this time his fingers were gentle. He stroked her cheek and then leaned close enough to her lips that her breath caught. "At least now it's clear who you should fear," he said.

CHAPTER 27

Eden unlocked the door as quietly as she could. She wanted Jarrod to make it to the bathroom and get his nosebleed to stop before Sullivan saw him. Before Eden could scope out the room, Az's voice came from the couch.

"Everything go okay?" Az turned toward them and saw the blood. He jumped up from the couch, instantly on alert.

Eden pressed a finger to her lips. "Where's Sullivan?" she whispered.

He nodded toward the kitchen as Sullivan came into the living room.

Jarrod's sigh ended in a gurgle. "It looks way worse than it is," he said, tilting his head up to pinch the bridge of his nose. The blood that had pooled in his hand rolled down his face, dripping onto the floor. Sullivan screamed.

Eden turned to Az. "Ice? Grab a wet towel, too." He was in the kitchen before she finished.

"My God, what happened?" Sullivan asked, rushing to him.

He sucked in a bubbly breath. "It's just a broken nose."

Eden almost laughed at the look Sullivan shot him. The girl gave good glare.

"And a split lip and one hell of a swollen cheek. I can see that. I didn't ask what it was; I asked what happened," Sullivan said. She touched his face gently.

Az bumped Eden from behind.

She grabbed the wet towel from him when Sullivan reached out. Her eyes met Eden's.

"I've got this," Sullivan said. "What happened?"

"You have to stop the bleeding first," Eden cut in. She held the towel on his nose and clamped Sullivan's hand down on top of it. "There," she said. "Tight."

Jarrod winced at the pressure. "I made a friend who wanted my wallet. I decided not to be his friend after all," he deadpanned.

Sullivan rocked back. "So you met Vaughn and got your ass kicked. I hope you at least got in a few punches, because you look like shit."

"Don't be too hard on his ego. It was a setup." Eden saw Az startle and turned toward him. "We think. Madeline."

"Wait," Az said. "Madeline set up Jarrod to get beat? Why?"

Eden's eyes strayed to Sullivan. "Because she wants me

to kill Vaughn. And I guess I seem like the vengeful type."
She wondered if it was as obvious as it seemed.

"Did you?" Az asked.

The opportunity had been right there to end two problems, kill Vaughn and get Madeline off her back. Eden
shook her head. "I can't do that anymore."

She glanced up, and Az smiled consolingly.

A buzzer sounded. They all spun toward the call box
beside the door.

Sullivan's hand dropped. "It's not him, is it?"

Without the pressure, a stream of red flowed out of
Jarrod's nose. Sullivan reached for his hand, but he pulled
away. A hurt expression clouded her eyes as she went back
to holding his nose.

Jarrod caught it. "I'm sorry. I've got no gloves on," he
said softly.

Az pressed the button on the intercom. "No entry without appointment," he said in a formal voice. They waited
through the long pause. "Probably hit the wrong—"

"I wasn't aware. Please forgive me, but it's an
emergency."

Eden swore as the voice came through the speaker.
"Buzz him in, Az." He paused for a second, confused by
her reaction. "It's Sebastian. Let him in. Now."

"Kristen's Sebastian?" Az pressed the button again.
"Identify yourself."

"Az, stop fucking around." Eden pushed him out of the way and hit the buzzer herself. "He hardly leaves the house. And Madeline said Kristen's been acting bizarre."

A knock sounded on the door. Sebastian had obviously run up the stairs. Something was wrong. Eden prepared herself for the worst, and swung it open.

Sebastian looked much the same as Eden remembered him from the day she'd left Kristen's, his black hair buzzed short. But usually he carried himself almost like he'd been through boot camp. Now he looked uncertain, his broad shoulders heaving.

"My apologies for the inconvenience," Sebastian said, awkwardly formal. Too much time around Kristen had rubbed off on him. Sebastian kept his eyes on her, his jaw set, his body tense. *He's terrified of me*, she realized. "I'm sorry to come unannounced. I didn't have a number for you. I need to talk to you."

He took in the scene around him—Jarrod bleeding all over himself, Sullivan doing her best to stop the flow.

Eden gestured to the couch. "Okay, talk."

"In confidence," Sebastian added.

"We are in confidence."

Sebastian shifted, clearly uncomfortable with the crowd. Eden didn't care. Everybody present she could trust except Sebastian himself.

She could see him weighing his need for her help and

his desire not to have whatever he'd come to say heard by others. "I'm not sure. I'm not even sure I should have come. She'd be angry if she knew I was here."

He finally brought himself to sit on the threadbare couch. "She's . . . she's not been well for a while. You know there's something wrong with her. She tries to hide it, but it's always been there. There was a guy. I only saw him officially twice. Once, the day before you left." He paused, as if it were a memory he knew neither of them wanted to recall. "And once *with* you." He looked up, met her eye. *Gabriel,* she realized.

"Go on."

His eyes darted around the apartment again, lingering on Az as if sizing him up.

"There are patterns to her . . . behavior. She seems like herself for a few weeks and then starts to spend more time in her room. She becomes frustrated, distant, and confused. And soon after, *he* shows up. And then things go back to normal. For a while, anyway."

"And he stopped showing up, didn't he?" When she looked up, Sebastian stared back at her with suspicion. Eden licked her lips. She didn't want to tell him what was wrong with Kristen. It was information Sebastian should have had, and Eden knew it wouldn't sit well. Kristen's formality had worn off on Sebastian; he'd clearly picked up her paranoia, too. "How is she?"

"She was getting worse." He paused.

Her head snapped up. "*Was* getting worse?"

He nodded once. "Was. Kristen didn't come home last night. The night before last, I heard voices coming from her room. I hadn't even known she was home until she texted me demanding privacy." He dropped his eyes. "I broke her wishes. I saw someone."

"Who did you see, Sebastian? The same guy from before?"

Sebastian's hands gripped his knees. "Dark," he whispered, shuddering. "Strange and dark. I heard his boots on the back stairs when he left, and I looked out the back window."

Eden stilled. "What did he look like?" she asked slowly, already knowing what the answer would be.

"He had curly hair, black leather jacket, and carried a case. A guitar case."

"Fuck." Az turned away. He'd clearly come to the same conclusion as she had. Madeline's hunch had been right.

Jarrod brushed Sullivan's wet rag away from his cheek. "Wait, Luke? Luke has Kristen?" The blood that he hadn't managed to lose from his nose and cheek drained out of his face.

Sebastian's eyes skirted toward him, back to Eden. "She was there yesterday morning, but left early. I haven't seen nor heard from her since. It's unusual."

"How unusual," Eden asked, taking the wrapped ice from Az and switching it for the rag with Sullivan.

Sebastian hesitated. "Unheard of. Even on her worst days, we're in contact at least by text if she doesn't want to be disturbed."

Eden kept her face stoic. Madeline might not want to do anything, but if Kristen was sick, she needed help. "Looks like we're gonna have to go after her." She sat down on the couch, opened the laptop on the table, let it load. She typed in an address and clicked a link.

"Who is he?" Sebastian asked.

"He's a nightmare," Eden whispered. The room fell still. She glanced up at Az. "Luke's playing tonight. At Aerie. It'll catch him off guard to just show up."

Jarrod gulped. "Eden, I . . ."

"You're not going," Eden said reassuringly. "You're going to stay here and watch over Sullivan."

"No."

"Jarrod," Eden snapped. She pointed at Sullivan. "I'm going with my gut, and my gut says you stay here with Sullivan."

Jarrod looked pained. Everything in him must have wanted to fight her on it, but with his terror at the mention of Luke she knew she couldn't put him through that again. Sullivan figured out enough to keep her mouth shut. Jarrod huffed but didn't fight, holding the ice on the goose egg rising off his cheek.

"Thank you," Sullivan said quietly. Eden met her eye. She wasn't sure what she was being thanked for. Leaving Jarrod out of a fight that was clearly going to be dangerous, maybe even making sure Sullivan wasn't doing any more Touch. Either way, Eden gave her a nod. Let Jarrod keep his pride. Keep him safe. God knew Eden wasn't exactly ecstatic to be facing Luke again.

Even less about telling Az he wouldn't be going, either.

CHAPTER 28

Jarrod squinted, his black eye puffy enough to be distracting. His cheekbone stung like hell, but he kept still while Sullivan started to clean him up. Eden, Az, and Sebastian had gone to check the alley for Vaughn.

Neither of them spoke about it. Sullivan dipped the washcloth under the running faucet and squeezed it out. She'd gotten half of his face done, was getting ready to start the side with the split across his cheek. His jaw throbbed.

She stood back, frowning as she gave his face a once-over. Gently, she touched a finger to his chin, turned his head. "God, you're a mess," she whispered. "Take off your shirt."

He pulled the ruined work uniform over his head, wondered if he'd ever need it again anyway. The undershirt was just as wrecked. He tossed them both into the tub. "You should see the other guy," he tried, but she didn't seem to find the humor in it.

"Vaughn's a big guy. I'm guessing he started it?"

Jarrod shrugged.

She ran the washcloth down his hairline, working her way to his neck. Blood stained his skin in smears. "What'd he say?"

That you need serious help, he wanted to say, *that I'm not gonna be able to save you.* But he shook his head instead. "Doesn't matter. He was wrong."

"That bad, huh?" She dropped the bloody cloth into the sink and cranked on the water, leaning against the porcelain basin.

"How did you meet Vaughn?" he asked suddenly.

She stared at him for a second before she managed to recover. "I was out with my friends looking for Touch. He sold to us. I ended up hanging out with him a few times, and we hit it off." She squeezed the hot water out of the cloth and dabbed softly at his upper lip. "I thought I already told you that?"

"You did," he said quietly, knowing his voice wasn't as casual as he wanted it to be, plowing ahead anyway. "When?"

"When did I meet him or when did I tell you?"

"Meet him." Jarrod swiped at the water dripping down his neck.

Sullivan's brow furrowed, her eyes on the ceiling as she thought. "Six months ago, I guess?"

You knew she wouldn't remember anyway, he thought. *She's not lying even if he was telling the truth.* Jarrod leaned forward, head down, his elbows balanced on his knees. "Did he seem, like, familiar when you met him?"

He felt the pressure of the cloth against the back of his neck as she cleaned the last of the blood.

"Familiar how?"

He rose up and caught the confusion in her look. "Forget it," he said, glancing away as he got to his feet. "You know that I'm . . . I mean, about how I'm not . . ."

Sullivan raised an eyebrow. "Alive?" she filled in.

He tried to smile and felt the split in his lip separate again. She wiped at it with her thumb.

"So you have a thing for dead boys or what?"

"Are you kidding me? Half the movies out there these days are about girls getting with vampire guys or werewolf guys or some other supernatural hotness. I'm living the dream." She sighed, a fake dreamy sound. "Lucky me. The envy of thirteen-year-olds coast-to-coast."

His shoulders shook. He fought to keep the laugh from his broken lip.

He meant to thank her for cleaning him up, but when he opened his mouth what came out was different. "You'd tell me, right? If you were feeling like you did." He paused. "On the roof."

He moved his hands to her shoulders, forced her to

look at him. "How often do you get like that, Sullivan?"

Her eyes told him everything he needed to know.

"What did Vaughn say to you?" she whispered.

He pulled her into a hug, sighed against her hair. Now that he was closer to her, he could feel the heat coming off her. "Jesus!" he said, holding her at arm's length. "Did you take anything for that yet?"

When she stepped back, he saw the glassy sheen to her eyes, not sure if it was the fever or tears, if he'd missed it before. "It's nothing," she said.

He opened the medicine cabinet and handed her a bottle of pain relievers. "Take, like, three of them. Your brain's gonna fry if you don't get that down."

She turned the bottle in her hand, the pills rattling slowly. "Sure you can trust me after what Vaughn told you?"

Jarrod grabbed the bottle of Tylenol, twisted off the cap, and shook out enough for both of them. He dropped a few to Sullivan, careful of his bare fingertips, tossed back a trio himself, and slugged them down with a palm full of water. It tasted like blood. He held his hand to his mouth, stifled a gag, sure he felt a thick slosh in his stomach.

"What's going on with Eden's friend? She didn't want you going with her."

"Eden didn't want me there because of Luke," he answered, his face still twisted with the taste of iron.

"I take it he's your big, bad arch-nemesis?" she said.

Jarrod opened the medicine cabinet and put the bottle away, his face hidden from her behind the mirror. "Might say that." He swung it closed. "Come with me," he said, leading the way to the couch.

Sullivan plopped down beside him. On the coffee table the laptop was still open to Aerie's website, their schedule of bands for the next weeks. He clicked the link for Dawn's Supernova, waited while it redirected him to a video.

"This is Luke," he said while it buffered, frozen on a shot of Luke mid-stage and glowering straight at the camera. Unease ripped through Jarrod, ached in his bones, his organs. Even the blood in his veins seemed to curdle.

Sullivan's voice was uncertain. "A singer?"

The video kicked in and Luke's snarl filled the room. Jarrod jumped, snapped the laptop closed, embarrassed.

"I can't. . . ." He turned to Sullivan, not caring about his reaction, the shake in his hands, the crack in his voice. "You ever see him, you run. If I'm with you. If he has me. I don't care. Sullivan, you leave me and you run."

"Jarrod, what—"

"No. Promise me."

"I promise," she said, her eyes wide. "What happened? I mean, you walked in here half an hour ago covered in blood and didn't even seem fazed, but you're, like"—she took his trembling hand at the wrist—"you're shaking after watching two seconds of *video* with the guy?"

"He killed some . . ." How to explain what Adam had been to him? His friend? Even after what he'd done? "Some people who used to live here with us. He hurt Az really bad, Eden . . . me." He tipped his chin toward the closed laptop. "That's Hell. And the reason I don't do roofs." He didn't elaborate and, much to his relief, she didn't ask. He let the silence build between them.

CHAPTER 29

Glass crunched under Luke's boots as he paced, playing his guitar softly. He'd been practicing for an hour in the hidden room, backstage at Aerie, the notes falling from him as he walked.

The couch Kristen stretched on was cigarette burned, springs digging into her back. She was grateful she'd decided to wear black slacks, even if the tight bustier paired with them pinched a bit. Against her chest lay a volume of poetry. The pages smelled of the bookstore Luke had taken her to that afternoon. He'd bought her every book she'd laid a finger on until she'd forgotten about the doomsayer, the Bound. Everything but him.

She snuck glances at Luke, small sips. The light in the dank room was weak, meant for showing off the tattered posters decorating the walls. And still, it caught his body. The perfect curve of his shoulders as he adjusted the strap of his guitar. The swagger of his hips as he moved.

Halfway through the song he sung, he shifted to practicing scales, his fingers slipping down the frets. "You're watching me," he said suddenly.

She paused, her smile unsure. In truth, the book she held was a prop. She hadn't been able to read a word with Luke's lyrics rolling over her.

"At the risk of feeding your ego, I rather like your singing. You're putting Yeats to shame." She closed the book. Luke chuckled as he lifted the guitar over his head. "Oh, hush," she said. "It was a tiny little thing of a compliment."

He propped the guitar against a broken speaker. "Better than Yeats? Coming from you, that's almost an attempt at seduction, Kristen."

With each stride toward her, the frenzy in his eyes intensified. Lust and need and danger. Her heart skipped quick beats in her chest. She flipped the book back open, trying to ignore him. "We both know my powers of seduction far outweigh yours. Only I don't play them as fast and loose."

He crawled over the armrest and onto the couch. The smell of spices filled her head. "Prove it," he challenged.

He snatched the book from her and laid it on the floor beside them. When she moved to pick it up, his fingers ran the length of her arm. Kristen shivered.

"See, I barely need to touch you. Where's your control?"

he chastised. "You used to be such a minx, Kristen."

"*My* control?" Kristen stared him down, knowing he only did it to bait her. But the chance to catch him off guard, put him in his place, was too tempting. She raised an eyebrow, giving his shoulder a gentle push. Luke followed the momentum, let himself fall back against the armrest.

"You'd give in so easily?" he asked. She sat up and tipped forward, sliding a leg across his leather pants until she straddled him. He hadn't expected her to respond. That much was clear. She added a twist to her hips as she settled.

"I'm not giving." She arched her back, one palm pressed against his abs, the other rising to catch the ribbon she'd used to tie up her hair. In one smooth movement she yanked it free and shook the strands loose. "I'm taking what I want."

She slipped the tips of her fingers under the waistband of his pants, teasing. "You did say that's proper etiquette Downstairs?"

She grazed his neck with her teeth, each tiny bite ending with the soft press of her mouth against his skin.

"Holy Hell, Kristen." His voice was breathless.

She thought about ripping the shirt off him. How far could she go before stopping would become impossible? Already, she knew she treaded the line, the gasp that escaped him sending a tremble through her body. His hips rose, pressing against her. She clutched the back of his neck, kneading the tight muscles there as she drew herself closer. Her lips found his earlobe. Beneath her, his whole body lifted in anticipation, wanting her.

Exactly where she wanted him.

"I win," she whispered. With a breathy laugh, she pulled back.

Luke caught her wrist.

She looked down, surprised by the roughness of his grip, the intensity in his eyes burning through her. In a flash he sat up, his hands at her waist, rolling her until she was under him. Shock stole her air. Each breath darkened his eyes until they blazed black as pitch. His hands pushed down on her shoulders, his body atop hers.

"Should I take what *I* want?" He slid his finger down to the button of her pants. It popped loose.

"Stop." She couldn't break away from his eyes, the darkness eating her up. Part of her wanted to let it. "Luke, I said stop!" she yelled, yanking an arm free. Her palm cracked hard against his cheek. The force of the slap turned his face from her.

He froze. And then his hands lifted away.

"It's dangerous to lure me into games, Kristen," he said quietly.

"No harm done." She touched his reddened cheek. A muscle twitched in his jaw.

Luke untangled himself from her and sat up. The play was gone from his eyes.

"I want you," he said, "to choose me this time. I'll give you happiness. Books. Pleasure. Anything you wish," he promised.

His mouth moved slowly toward hers and she thought for a moment that he'd forgotten the danger of her lips, but he moved to her jaw and the side of her neck, leaving a trail of goose bumps that did nothing to slow her speeding pulse.

"Why? Why me?"

He trailed his fingers down her face and then further. They lingered against the swell of her breast, the lace of her bustier. "Because you tempt me. You demand I fight for your affections instead of taking what I please." He dropped his hand. "You tell me no. You say stop. And I listen." He said the last words like a curse, anger bleeding through, each word rougher than the last.

Luke tilted his head, his neck tense, cracking with a snap. He rolled his shoulders.

"You're a silly little dead girl." He glared at her, his tone harsh. "You should mean exactly nothing to me." He grabbed her chin, forced her to meet his eyes. "And yet I covet you more than anything else on this Earth."

He was off the couch and across the room before Kristen could react. She rose to her knees in time to catch the opening of the door.

It closed and cut off the sound of even his receding footsteps. Left her somehow hating the silence she'd always welcomed.

CHAPTER 30

Eden grabbed her gloves, reached for a scarf and decided against it. It didn't seem very bright to put something around her neck that he could choke her with.

"Are you ready?" she asked Sebastian, coming out of her room. They'd agreed to head out to Aerie early. If they could catch Luke off his game, maybe he'd slip up a bit. Not that it was likely.

"Yes," Sebastian said instantly. Eden nodded. From the corner of her eye she saw Az stand.

She turned to him. "You're not coming."

He froze with his hand in mid-reach for his coat, a perfect statue of confusion before his expression turned to disbelief. "You can't be serious."

She kept her eyes on him. "I'm dead serious. You're staying here, Az."

"Not a fucking chance, Eden." He yanked his coat down.

"Az." She moved closer, putting her hands on his shoulders. "Listen to me, all right? Listen." He shook his head, but she went on anyway. "Luke will do whatever it takes to get to you." She searched his eyes, letting him see the fear in hers, not hiding it. "If you're there, I'll be concentrating on you. I need to be able to watch my back, right?"

His jaw tightened, the muscles working. She met his gaze, the hurt in it torturous.

"I need you here. I need someone to play the hero if this goes bad," she said, dropping her eyes. "And I know you'll come for me."

He winced, then nodded. She forced herself to turn away, leave while she could. "Let's go," she said to Sebastian as she pulled the door open and pounded down the stairs.

"Eden! Wait!"

She wanted to keep going, but found herself turning around. Az rushed down the stairs, slowing as he got closer.

"Be careful," he whispered. He pulled her into a tight hug, his lips on her ear. "I love you and please don't . . . please be careful."

Suddenly, he lifted his head, his eyes on Sebastian. "Anything happens, you run. First thing you do is call me." Sebastian nodded. "Give him my number," Az added to Eden. She lifted her arms and wrapped them around Az. "Be fast," he said.

A few early fangirls wandered aimlessly in front of the club, chain-smoking, but at an hour and a half before the opening band would take the stage, the place was fairly deserted. Sebastian grabbed Eden's arm as they approached, but his eyes stayed on the door, eager and angry, ready to fight for Kristen. "Anything in particular I should know?"

"Yeah. He hates me."

Sebastian's brow wrinkled.

"Jarrod threw Luke off a roof. After I killed his girl-friend," she finished, striding up to the door.

She tried the handle first, found it locked, and slammed her hand against the wood. Her palm was almost bleeding by the time someone finally opened it. Smears of gray ash graffitied the door. She ignored them. As long as the pain held off, she'd be fine.

"Is there a fucking problem?" the guy barked. "Doors open an hour before the show!"

"No." The word crackled with enough quiet authority that the bouncer didn't interrupt her. "We're here to see Luke. Now."

He checked her out, one eyebrow raised, assessing. Apparently, she failed the test. "That only works in the movies. Nice try, though," he said, the door starting to fall shut.

"You want to tell him Eden's here. Trust me," she called through the crack. Crossing her arms, she leaned against the wall, waiting. On the sidewalk, a pair of girls giggled, whispering about her behind their hands. She gave them a satisfied grin when the door opened again thirty seconds later.

"He's finished sound check," the guy said sheepishly, leading them across the empty dance floor, headed to the backstage door. Eden stopped halfway there.

She'd be damned if she was going to be locked in the tiny room with Luke again. She remembered it well, where she'd first met him. The stench of cigarette butts and spilled beer. The only door led to a back lot that offered no escape. "No. Tell him to come meet us out here."

"Jesus Christ, you're a pain in my ass," she heard him mutter as he went on to deliver her message.

"He *can* die, correct?" Sebastian said suddenly. "Because I will kill him if he's harmed her."

"I don't know," she said, flashing back to the nights she'd seen him onstage. His mere presence stoked crowds to a fever pitch. He fed off it, reveled. She wondered if he took his strength from those screams. "He might be weaker before a show."

"Eden?"

Sebastian startled at the voice, staring over Eden's shoulder. Eden heard the backstage door slam. She spun around in time to see Kristen's eyes go wide. "Sebastian, what are you doing here?" She balled her hands into fists. "Leave," she commanded. "Leave me alone. Now."

"Kristen, what on Earth are you doing? Come with us. No one has to know about any of this." Luke was nowhere in sight. A few more minutes and they'd be out the door. It was almost too easy. "We can set you up at my place. Obviously not your whole crew, but you and Sebastian." Her eyes flicked back to Kristen. "I'll do what I can to help you."

Kristen's face steeled. "Help? The way you helped Gabe?'"

Eden opened her mouth. No words came. Kristen knew about Gabe, and from the blaze of her eyes, she knew it was Eden's fault.

Sebastian stepped forward. "Kristen, come with us."

"Oh? You're giving orders now?"

His bravado seemed to break for a second before he recovered.

"Thank you," Kristen said, "for your offer. I won't be taking you up on it. You can leave now."

Eden snapped. "He's the fucking devil, Kristen. Gabe's Fallen and you're shacking up with Lucifer when we should be working together. Like we did before. Your

Touch helped me stop Luke from taking us all on the roof. Don't let him take *you* now."

"Hello, Eden."

A gasp slipped out of her before she could stop it, stole away whatever edge she'd managed to carve out. The soft baritone shredded her anger, left her unraveling. He was directly behind her, so close that she trembled. Still, she turned. Faced him. "We've come for Kristen," she said.

Luke had healed since the last time she'd seen him, bloody and broken from his fall off the roof. If anything, he looked stronger, more confident. "I figured. You were a little early for the show." He moved and Eden staggered back, realizing too late that he only moved past her to stand beside Kristen. "I don't believe she wants that."

"Kristen." Sebastian smiled when she turned to him, as if he needed proof she remembered who she was. "I know things must seem confusing right now." His voice took on the soft lilt of a therapist, fake comfort words. "Perhaps it's best if you come with us. There's discord at home. The Siders need your leadership."

Kristen scoffed. "Have you learned nothing from me, Sebastian?" She clasped Luke's hand as if for backup, though she looked unbreakable. "Keep them in line with cruelty, reward them with your kindness. If you can't manage a few Siders for a week, then I've wasted my time training you these years."

He winced at the blow.

Eden glared at Luke. "Did you force this on her?"

He laughed, the sound bouncing around the empty club. "You throw around orders and for once someone doesn't jump, so it must be a conspiracy. Kristen does have a mind of her own."

"Yes," Eden said, keeping her voice even. "A sick mind. She's not well right now."

Luke cocked his head, offended. "You say these things, talk to me like she's not right here, can't hear every word, and wonder why she hates you so?" She saw Kristen stiffen beside him. Luke raised her hand, kissing the knuckles, a clear flaunt of his prize, though Kristen's weak smile showed she didn't view it that way. "Let's go. You don't have to see them again."

"Wait!" Eden called as they headed back toward the stage. "What would Gabriel say, Kristen? How badly would it hurt him to see you with Luke?"

"He knows," Kristen said quietly. "He told me what he did to you. What Az was too weak to do himself. Gabe gave up everything for the two of you." Kristen shrugged, but emotion battled in her eyes. "Why would he ever care what happens to me?"

Eden shook her head. "Kristen, it's not—" The words caught her. "My God, you saw him? Where?"

"Stop it!" Kristen's outburst left her face scarlet. "I

can't save Gabriel. No one can. And it's *your* fault!"

"So you're whoring yourself out to the Fallen?" Eden screamed back.

Luke charged, his face suddenly an inch from Eden's. "It wasn't enough for you to take Gabe from her? You've decided to take away the only other person who bothered to help her. You think I'm going to stand aside?"

Luke's shoulder twisted as Sebastian grabbed it. His hand shot out, shoving Sebastian to the floor.

"Luke!" Kristen strode back to them, fearless. Eden flinched, waiting. Kristen would give the command, have Luke take her. "Leave them."

Luke's eyes stayed on Eden, his face close enough that his angry breaths hit her cheek. "You gave up on Gabriel the moment he Fell. You hate her for doing what she needed to stay healthy without him. Tell me, Eden. Will you turn your back on Az soon? He's struggling. Have you even noticed, or are you really that wrapped up in yourself?"

Hearing Az's name come from him was enough to spark her rage. "Is getting Kristen your revenge for what I did to Libby?" she jeered, knowing the blow had struck true when Luke's smarmy smile faded. "Yeah, remember Libby, your girlfriend? Looks like you moved on pretty quick there. But since she's Downstairs, I imagine you're splitting your time between her and Kristen," she said sweetly.

Kristen moved suddenly, put herself in front of Luke as if she were protecting him. "My utter *contempt* for you right now aside, you're wasting your time, Eden. I'm not leaving with you. You have nothing to offer me."

Sebastian shifted forward. "I've offered you my loyalty for years now. Trust me enough to come with me, Kristen."

Her face changed at Sebastian's words. "No," she said, but this time it was a whisper, uncertain. She took a step away from Luke, her eyes flicking back and forth as she hovered between him and Sebastian.

Luke took her hand. "I'm the dark you've always craved, Kristen. I need your light." He drew his thumb down her cheek to her jaw, curled across her chin. "Stay."

"Kristen, you can't possibly be buying this?" Eden asked in disbelief.

Kristen's stare was fixated on Luke.

Sebastian tried to grab her arm, but she pulled away. "You're better than being with someone who wants you to be dependent on *him* to be your best. Are you not seeing how he's manipulating you?" he demanded, his intensity surprising Eden.

"You think I'm manipulating her? That I wouldn't grant her every whim?" Luke toyed with the rings on Kristen's hand.

Eden laughed bitterly. Inside her chest, her heart

hammered, her brain humming with things Madeline had told her—that she would try to press Luke, see if there were some way to get Gabe Bound again. "It doesn't matter, Luke." *Work,* she thought. *Please work.* "You'll always know if it were an option, Kristen would have chosen Gabriel."

Luke froze as her words hit him. "It doesn't matter." He tried to work up his smile, but it faltered. He turned to Kristen. "Do you want the choice?"

Kristen gave her head a slight shake. "What are you saying, Luke?"

His face hardened, confidence pulling back his shoulders. "I won't be your second choice." Eden held her breath as Luke smiled at her. "They go by the books Upstairs, and Eden's not on the books. You can't murder someone who doesn't exist."

Kristen raised a hand, clutching her chest in disbelief. "What are you saying?" she demanded.

"If someone were to go Upstairs and point out that little loophole, they'd have to let Gabriel back."

Eden couldn't move, couldn't breathe. Gabe would be Bound again; Kristen wouldn't need Luke. Az would be safe. "And you'll tell them? The Bound?" Eden managed, her heart racing.

Luke scoffed. "I'm Fallen, Eden. It's not like they sent me off with a set of day passes."

Disappointment flooded her. "Then what does it matter? We can't get Upstairs."

Luke smiled. "*You* can't. No one can but the Bound. Or," he added slowly, "those who have an open invitation in the form of a pair of pretty wings."

Eden's breath choked off. The room tunneled. She tried to shake it off, make sense of what he said. Az. Az could save Gabe?

Kristen dropped back into Luke's arms. She stared at Eden, heat in her glare. "You'd better help Gabriel. You owe me that much."

Luke smiled at Eden over Kristen's shoulder before he pulled away and took Kristen's hand, walking toward the backstage door.

Just before they reached it, he turned back.

"Oh, and Eden? Az already knows. He's known the whole time."

CHAPTER 31

Sebastian stayed quiet beside her, staring awkwardly out the window of the cab while Eden fought to control her rage. By the time they reached the apartment, it was a tightly wound ball inside her. She took the stairs slowly, dreading every one, knowing what came at the top. Sebastian didn't follow her up.

She opened the door. Az leaped up from the couch when she came in, relief on his face. He covered the ground between them in seconds, caught her in his arms.

The tight squeeze stole her breath.

"Are you all right?" He kissed her neck, his hands gripping tight around her waist. Eden didn't move. "Where's Kristen?" he asked, confused. "Where's Sebastian?"

She wanted to react. To call up the rage she'd felt in the cab, the heartbreak. Nothing was left. Nothing.

"You don't want to save Gabe," she said. The words sounded flat and hollow in the empty room. She didn't know where Jarrod and Sullivan were, didn't ask.

Az's fingers stopped just before brushing against her skin. "Eden, what happened at Aerie?"

"All you have to do is tell the Bound I wasn't mortal when he killed me. I'm not on record. That's all you have to do." She whispered the last bit, the words slow. "Did you know?" She looked up at him, his hand frozen near the side of her face, lips parted with denials still shaping.

"Wait, who told you this? Luke?" He stepped away from her. "Eden, it's a trick. It's not that easy."

She followed him. "You can go Upstairs and clear Gabriel's name. Michael was only trying to get you to help Gabe, wasn't he?"

Az's legs hit the back of the couch.

"You could save Gabriel and you choose not to." Fury found its way back into her. "Deny it."

He shook his head. "Eden, it's not—"

"Deny it!" she screamed, a hot tear rushing down her cheek. "You tell me I'm wrong. You tell me you'd never be capable of doing something this awful, this evil! You deny it, Az!"

He slumped against the armrest of the couch. "I can't."

"Why?" she yelled. "What the hell is wrong with you?"

Az turned from her. His fist slammed into the wall, the clock rattling before it fell, breaking when it hit the floor. "Stop asking, Eden! You know what's wrong with me! The same thing that's always been wrong with me!"

"Gabe was there for you for years! He sacrificed everything he knew for you. Now he needs you to help him. And you're trying to tell me you won't swallow your fucking pride and clear his name! Use the wings!"

He flexed his hand, his knuckles already bruising. He kept his eyes on the floor. "It's his revenge on us," he whispered. "Of course he'd tell you I could go."

He slumped, his voice dead as he explained. "I can't get in unless I'm Bound, Eden. So I use the wings to get there. And then I take an oath. I give up everything down here. I become one of them again. Shackled to duty. Doing their bidding." He glanced up. "It's got nothing to do with pride. They won't let me back here."

"No," she whispered. Too easy, she'd thought, when Luke had told her. And now the terrible twist cut through her.

"I lose the wings, I lose you." Az took her hand.

"But can't Michael just—"

"They need a witness, someone who was there, to testify. That's why Michael wanted me. He needs me." His face clouded. "If I'm Bound again, they won't trust me to come back here."

"Why didn't you tell me?" she asked, her voice small.

"Because I was afraid." His eyes deepened to the bluest blue. He didn't bother keeping the pain from his voice. "I was afraid you would want me to go anyway."

"So you kept it from me. You lied." She swiped her hand across her cheek, barely noticing the black on her fingers when she lowered them. "I used to see the good in you."

She closed her eyes, couldn't even look at him.

"Eden, please. Don't do this." A soft, broken sound escaped him. "I didn't know what else to do."

She slid her hand out of his. "You could have told the truth. You could have trusted me. You could have kept your promises."

"I promised you I'd stay," he said.

A sharp stab dug through her chest. She thought at first it was her heart, but then it worsened. She hissed a breath.

"You're sick again, aren't you?" He brushed his thumb across the side of her neck. "You said the pain was nothing."

"It'll pass. I just need . . ."

"What's happening to you?" His eyes were wide and frightened.

"I don't know." Everything was falling apart. Even her.

"Eden, I don't think this is a normal thing," he whispered.

She couldn't get enough of a breath to answer him. She doubled over, a scream nearly silenced behind her clenched teeth. Her legs gave out and the cry burst free.

"Eden!" He brushed the tears from her cheeks, his fingers dripping black as ink. "Oh God," he whispered, staring at her face in horror. She didn't want to know what he saw.

It'll stop. Any second. She bore down, waiting for the release, but the pain only intensified. She felt his hands, thought he was trying to figure out where she hurt, but then the hands were gone again and she heard the tones of him sending a call on her phone.

"Eden, breathe!" She couldn't, ashes clogging her windpipe. She mouthed his name, reaching for him. "Madeline," he yelled into the phone. "It's Eden; something's wrong. I don't know—"

He cut off and Eden forced herself to focus. "Yes, there's black on her face, all over her hands." His breath caught in a hitched panic. "Fuck, Madeline, ashes are coming out of her eyes!" He cuffed his sleeve around his fingers, gently wiping her face. "Stay with me," he murmured as he listened to whatever Madeline said. "You have to kill the Siders, Eden. This is happening because you stopped."

She shook her head.

"What if she won't?" he said into the phone. The color drained from Az's face. He grabbed for Eden's hand as she finally managed a hacking cough of air. "She won't send them Downstairs, Madeline." His eyes met Eden's.

"But she would if her Siders went Upstairs, if Gabe were Bound again."

She gasped hard, trying to pull in enough air to speak, her head shaking wildly. Az dropped the phone. It clacked against the floor and spun away. She could hear Madeline screaming for him but couldn't make out the words.

"I can fix this." Az stared down in a daze, as if putting a puzzle together. His hands cupped Eden's face, forcing her to stop thrashing. Certainty shone in his eyes. "I can do this."

"Az, no!" she blurted. "Wait!" He ripped away from her hold on him and ran for the door.

She screamed as he took off through it. Her eyes clouded over black.

She rubbed them furiously, heard his steps slam down the stairs. She fumbled blindly for the railing. "Az!" she cried.

She froze, waited for him to answer, to come back.

"I love you," he whispered. The stairwell fell silent, and then Eden heard the twist of the doorknob.

The click as it closed.

CHAPTER 32

Gabe could smell the cooking meat. In the distance an orange glow ran along the broken horizon line, the flames hidden from view by rolling hills. Barren trees stretched into the dark sky. A low drone hummed through his bones, the far-off sound of uncountable screams carried up his legs through the dirt and ash below his feet. Cages hung, hundreds of them on J-shaped hooks protruding from the ground, holding them aloft like oversized aviaries. Each one held a single drenched prisoner. Droplets streaked down Gabe's own face, the drizzle slowly soaking him through.

"Raining in Hell," he mumbled.

A crackling hiss of steam squelched out with each of his steps, the ground breaking apart, exposing the smoldering earth to the moisture. Gabe's teeth chattered as he tried to focus, to remember.

Her lips are cracked. When she licks them, her tongue

is black. Around him the cages swung wildly, struggling arms and shoulders wrenching through the bars and stretching toward him. A dozen voices begging for bare flesh. Pleading to touch him.

Siders. Touch didn't work Downstairs as it did on Earth. Here, within a few hours of being passed Touch, the victim disintegrated. Vanished. Luke had caught them and put them here, trying to quarantine the plague their fingertips spread through Downstairs souls.

Her hair, long and streaked with dirt, hides her from him. I can't kill them, she moans.

Gabe kept his eyes down. He couldn't look at them, the Siders driven mad, delirious. On Earth, Touch wouldn't work on an angel. Here, though, rumors swirled. Other Fallen had gone missing. The souls trapped for eternity in Hell were blinking out of existence. No one came near the Siders. No one but Gabe.

Find her. Gabe walked among the desiccated limbs, out of the Siders' reach. *A cough of dust. Black tears.* Any cage that rattled wasn't the one he searched for.

"Gabriel." A tremor passed through him at the name. He swiveled to the cage beside him.

She hung there, her eyes wide, sightless and soot filled. Muddy tears streaked down her cheeks. She crawled closer, the tips of her fingers crumbling away as she struggled to the bars. "Gabriel? Is it . . ." she gasped, and choked out a cough. Over the moans of the Siders around them, he heard her wheezed inhales.

He reached into the cage, fingers trailing the gentlest touch on her shoulder. "It's me, Libby."

She shuddered and collapsed against the bars, the effort of moving exhausting her. He glanced around at the other cages, the Siders in them. None of them suffered Libby's fate.

"You're so much worse," he whispered. He brushed her hair back from her face, layers of her cheek sloughing off and falling to ash. His eyes darted to the other Siders. They were insane with the buildup of Touch, but none of them were sick, not like Libby. She held out a shaky hand in their direction.

"They don't spread Touch and it builds in them. I don't spread death and . . . If I could just kill one . . ." She hacked, small gray clots spraying from her lips as she fought to draw a breath. She'd told him before that her power, the same one Eden had, didn't work. Perhaps there was no soul to send on, but whatever the reason, the Siders Downstairs were immune to her lips. She couldn't kill them, even if she hadn't been caged.

Her wet clothes clung to her. Gabe stripped off his coat and fed it through the bars, carefully spreading it over her. He thought of Eden, tied to him because he'd taken her life. She had prided herself on sending the Siders Upstairs, neither of them knowing she infected Heaven with every one. He wondered if the Bound had caught on yet, what they were doing to eradicate Touch. *One upside to being Fallen,* he thought. *Eden's not infecting Upstairs anymore.*

The rain shifted from drizzle to downpour, plinking against the metal. Gabe shuddered, tiny hailstones prickling his skin. All around them the ground groaned and steamed.

Libby swiped a hand around under the coat. "Take it off," she murmured.

She's delirious, he thought. "Libby, you're shivering. The coat will keep you warm."

"No," she said. Her arm flopped forward. Hail pelted against it, chipping away pieces of her skin. She writhed, a weak cry of pain breaking from her. Ashy gray rivulets ran from her palms. She was falling apart, crumbling like charcoal. "I said," she whispered, "take it off. Please." From under the thick wool, her eyes shone black and leaking. "Please, Gabriel."

He couldn't bear to look, turned from her. She heard his movement and struggled under the coat.

"Don't leave me like this," she pleaded with the last of her strength. Deep inside him a fire ignited, burning like the flames that still glowed brightly past the hills. "Please help me."

It was barely a whisper. He wondered how long it

would be before she broke apart on her own, fell to ash and scattered through the bars. As if in answer, she rasped a choked sob. Not long now.

His stomach turned at the thought of ending her pain instead of drawing it out, clenched hard enough that he went down on one knee. When he looked up, Libby's lips moved silently, between the bars of her prison, shaping a single word again and again.

Please.

Gabe reached through the bars and tugged the coat off her. Drops slammed against her, melted her away layer by layer. Libby moaned once more. The Siders around him screamed, rattling the locked doors of their cages. Sudden pain ripped through his veins like kerosene. He fell to the spongy ground, a convulsion yanking his head back, his body seizing.

Light burned white hot against his eyelids.

"A Fallen showing mercy?" a voice demanded, sounding smug and satisfied in a way that made Gabe's skin crawl. "Impossible."

"He should never have been one of them," another answered.

Gabe curled into a ball, dimly aware that the hail had stopped. *No*, he thought, *not stopped*. Under him wasn't smoldering earth, but white tile. It radiated heat, slowly warming him. He flattened every part of himself against the ground, basking.

"He's Bound again. That's all that matters." This voice, Gabe recognized.

He forced his eyes open.

Az didn't smile. "Find her. She needs you. Something's wrong." His voice cracked with emotion, his eyes piercing. "Help her, Gabriel?"

Behind him, a door opened. Shadowed figures filed in. The hooded cloaks they wore were stark white, their faces blank of features. Empty canvases save for a slit of a mouth.

"Azazel," one of them hissed. Az glanced behind him. When he turned back to Gabriel, fear yellowed his eyes.

"Gabe . . ." He sounded so broken, so absolutely shattered. "Remind me about her?"

Gabe sat up, realizing for the first time where he was. What it meant. "Az," he whispered. "What have you done?"

Those who stood around him gripped his wrists. Az staggered backward, a dozen sets of hands drawing him out the door.

CHAPTER 33

Kristen sat on the edge of the empty stage, swinging her legs. The club had almost cleared out. Luke was at the bar, signing a few last autographs. She watched him chatting amicably, the flirty smile he wore for the girls swooning over him. She didn't feel any jealousy. The looks he gave them were not the ones he'd given her, his eyes flicking her way through the show, the desire in his gaze searing her.

She flushed at the memory, smiling as she dropped her head, playing with her rings. And tonight . . .

"Kristen."

She looked up, toward Luke, but he had his back to her, an arm slung against the mirrored pillar he leaned against.

"Kristen." She snapped toward stage left, saw the curtain move, the shadows shift. She hauled her legs back over the edge of the stage, took a step toward the voice.

"Who's there?"

The curtain rustled again, a hand curled around the material.

He moved into the light.

"Gabriel!" Her shoulders heaved and her hand clamped over her mouth. Her eyes flashed to Luke, but he hadn't heard.

"Hi, sweetheart." Gabe held out his arms.

She couldn't help herself—her feet rushed toward him. He caught her in his arms, rocked them both into the darkness backstage, out of sight. Then he set her down and took her in.

"Kristen, I'm so sorry." She stepped back.

"You left me all alone." Her voice had a bite to it, a cruelness that he wouldn't see as an act as long as she kept her face in the shadows. "You tossed away our friendship so Eden would be safe a few days sooner. Days, Gabriel."

She lowered her voice, couldn't keep the bitterness from it. "Don't worry yourself, though. I managed without you."

"You played him brilliantly."

Her pause lasted for only a moment before she realized she no longer cared what he thought. "I didn't play him."

A slow clap startled her. Luke stood, center stage, a smile on his face. A pair of spotlights flared to life, one highlighting him, the other her and Gabriel. They shaded their eyes from the sudden glare.

"Bravo. You're quite the actor, Gabriel." Luke's voice echoed eerily though the silent club. "But the role of the hero's already been cast. You failed her and I won her heart. My comedy and your tragedy."

Gabriel stepped out from behind the curtain.

"She's not one of your toys, Lucifer. You can't use her for your own amusement. I won't allow it."

Luke laughed.

"He's not using me." Kristen moved closer to Luke. "He's been there for me. When you abandoned me, it was *Luke* who came to me. Who kept me from losing myself. Only Luke. This isn't the first time, either. He's proven himself."

Gabe's face grew grim. "He's not who you think he is."

"You're pathetic." Her voice raised an octave. "You wouldn't even be Bound again if it wasn't for him!"

She waited for the shock to hit him.

She heard Luke approaching her, drawing closer. "You don't know him like I do, Gabriel," she said fiercely.

"You're a plague, Kristen."

She fought back an angry laugh. "How poetic."

Gabe shook his head. "No, the Siders. The Siders are a plague, an infection."

Kristen glanced at Luke, unsure why his eyes burned Gabriel with silent fury. "Someone's been busy," Luke mused.

"I don't understand," she said, watching Gabriel's agitation compound. He reached for her again, but she moved her hand away. "What are you talking about?"

"The Siders that were sent on by Eden or Libby are still Siders. They're spreading Touch, but Down There it doesn't feed off feelings. It feeds off the *victim*. It's eating the souls. Disintegrating them. Do you think Luke would rather have that happening Upstairs or Down?" Pity shown in Gabriel's eyes. "He used you. He earned your favor, turned you against Eden and Az. He made you a pawn, Kristen, and he made it seem like saving me was a gift to you. A sacrifice. But it was what he wanted all along."

"That's not true," she said. "Why are you doing this to me?" *Earned your favor.* The words stuck in her head. Then Luke, the night he'd cashed in what she owed. *I want your favor. Your company.* She turned slowly to Luke. No, it was impossible. There was no way she would have been trapped in his snare so easily, played so perfectly. "You helped Gabriel for me. Because you love me."

His jet-black curls, still damp with sweat, blocked his eyes. "I want you. Covet you. More than you will ever know." He reached out to her. "Let that be enough."

She stared at his hand, but didn't take it. She lifted her eyes to his, recognizing the ferocity in them.

She made the slightest movement toward Gabe, but

didn't look away from Luke. "You used me."

"And you used me," he snarled. "I let you, didn't I? I *earned* your love." In a rush, he covered the steps between them. His hands whipped up, stopped short of touching her though she cried out anyway. Luke's lips brushed gently against her temple. "I can give you the world, Kristen." He ignored Gabriel's scoff. "This is everything you wanted."

She couldn't look at him, couldn't face the truth in what he said. "It was all a game."

"Don't you dare do this to me! I gave you this choice and you're using it against me?" His fingers curled, the calloused tips barely scratching her cheeks as he tightened them to fists. "You *chose* me!"

She lost herself, for one last moment, in his eyes. And then Kristen stepped back.

"I changed my mind."

He moved achingly slow, his chin sliding up her jaw-line, his lips to her ear. *He's going to tear me apart*, she realized. *He's going to torture the sanity out of me.* "Then walk away," he said, his voice dangerous but controlled. She didn't move, sure if she did he would strike. Instead, it was Luke who pulled away.

"Make your choice!" His words thundered through Aerie, echoing. "But be aware that there are consequences, Kristen."

She jumped as Luke pivoted sharply. He walked from the stage, taking the stairs down to the backstage door. The spotlight that had been shining on him shut off with a loud pop. The other followed.

"Are you okay?" Gabe called out, finding her in the near darkness.

"I don't know," she whispered. Her words broke the stillness, but barely.

Even as Gabriel helped her down and out of the club, her eyes stayed locked on the door Luke had disappeared behind.

CHAPTER 34

Eden swiped the tissue across her eyes, the skin stinging and raw. She sucked in a staggered breath. When she swallowed, she tasted blood and ash, her throat ragged. Her phone went off, vibrating across the table.

Nothing, it read when she flipped it open. Jarrod and Sullivan were out there together, searching, in case he hadn't gone through with it. Eden pressed Send on her phone, dialing through to Az.

"Please." She squeezed the phone against her ear, the screen hot from constant use. Beneath her, the floor was dusted over with thin, fragile flakes.

She hung up, hit Redial, black ashes scabbing from her fingertips.

At a frantic pounding on the door to the apartment, Eden dropped the phone and ran, only halfway there when it burst open. Her heart leaped into her throat before she saw Madeline.

"Madeline! Az is—"

"Tell me you didn't let him go!" Madeline screamed. Her eyes were wide, desperate. "He stayed, right? He's here?" She pushed past Eden instead of waiting for an answer, opening random doors.

She grabbed Eden's shoulders. "Why the fuck couldn't you have killed Vaughn like you were supposed to? It would have bought us time! If Gabe's Bound again, I'll destroy you."

Eden yanked away, stumbling. "You knew what was wrong with me? You knew we could save Gabriel, too, didn't you?"

Madeline grabbed her by the throat, tossed her to the floor. Eden cried out in pain, crumpling. "Of course I did!" Madeline paced the floor, wiping her hands clean from where she'd touched Eden. "Don't look at me like that," she sneered. "I tried to help you. It's not my fault you're all moral and stupid."

"I suppose I'm more collateral damage, right, Madeline? Like Kristen?"

Madeline threw back her head and laughed. "Kristen probably got the best deal out of any of us. *You* got totally screwed." She nudged Eden with her foot. "Get up. Come talk to me."

Madeline headed into the kitchen without waiting for Eden. She heard the fridge open, the snap of a soda can tab. Eden got to her feet, limped into the kitchen.

"You're dying." Madeline's eyes skimmed over her. "Christ, it's a miracle you're still here. I mean, one serious injury? Your body tries to use that Touch to heal and . . ." She raised her fist, splayed out the fingers. "Poof. Ashes to ironic ashes."

"That would have been great to know." Eden sat down at the table. "Especially when you were setting me up to get ambushed by Vaughn."

"Jarrod's a tough cookie. I delayed you enough for him to kick Vaughn's ass and give you an easy target. And how did you reward all my perfect strategizing?" She lifted the can, flicking her hand and sloshing the liquid inside. "Strolled right on by him, didn't you? He wasn't even conscious!"

"I won't send Siders to Luke," Eden said.

Madeline slammed the can to the table. "You're dead in days if you don't kill a Sider."

"I'm the only one of us like this. How would you have any clue what's happening to me?"

Madeline sipped her soda. "Because, Eden, it's how Luke is killing Libby."

"I sent her Downstairs." The pieces weren't coming together in Eden's mind.

"Exactly. And Luke realized all the Siders she had sent Downstairs were still spreading Touch. Only the Touch they spread killed off everything it infected. And what's Hell with no one to torture? He freaked. Locked up every Sider he could find, including Libby."

"How do you know this?" Eden demanded.

"Gabe. He's seen her. She's wasting away while all the others build up Touch and go mad. Libby's *dying*, Eden. For real, this time. But she *can't* kill the Siders, while you're just being a fucking martyr." Madeline set her can down on the counter. "Az knew how to save Gabe, but I thought the chance of him using the wings was miniscule. Turns out, you tell the boy his girlfriend's going Cinderella and he tunes out the important stuff."

Sorrow bubbled into Eden's chest, clouding her eyes. She waited to see if the pain would flare back. "He wanted to save me. Gabe, too."

"Az makes a terrible hero." Madeline snorted, the sound dying in her throat at the black tracks on Eden's cheeks. "You're tied to Gabriel. If he's Bound, your Siders will be infecting Upstairs. I imagine they won't find that idea too heartwarming. And the thing is, the Bound, well . . ." Her calculated breath made the wait even worse. "Now they know how to kill you."

CHAPTER 35

Snow crunched under Jarrod's feet. For hours they'd been canvassing Manhattan, though Jarrod knew it was only aimless wandering.

They'd ended up in Central Park, taking one path, then another, Sullivan's hand finding his as they walked. The woods around them were silent save for the snapping of frozen branches and soft patter of snow falling from the trees.

"What if we can't find him?" Sullivan asked.

Jarrod shrugged.

From the corner of his eye, he saw her studying him. "You don't think we're going to find him, do you?"

He shook his head. "No. I think Az is gone."

"So what are we doing in the park?"

He gave Sullivan a small smile. "You like to walk, and it's snowing. I figured we could both use some beautiful things."

She stopped, kissing him soft and slow. Her lips

lingered and he deepened the kiss, raised his hands to cup her face. Even through his gloves he could feel the heat radiating from her skin, though they'd been outside in the snow for hours. Her cheeks were mottled, splotched fiery red and white, her eyes glassy. Her fever was back and raging. "We should go back. You need to rest."

"I'm fine," she said, kissing him again. "It's only a fever."

He moved to turn them back around. Suddenly, she broke away. He thought she'd tripped, but when he looked over, he saw the arm wrapped around her neck.

"What a lovely night for a lovers' stroll," Luke said.

Jarrod froze, filled with fear. Sullivan clawed at the arm around her neck. Luke didn't seem to feel it.

"She's so pretty, Jarrod!" Luke ran his fingertips down Sullivan's cheek as he slammed a boot heel into the ground. The frozen puddle beneath him shattered. Wrapping Sullivan's hair around his hand, Luke reached down, grabbed an icy shard. "Has Eden told you about my style?" he asked with a smile. "How about Az? Did he ever tell you the stories of his past lovers? How I sliced off bits of them."

Sullivan gave a sharp cry.

Her voice jolted Jarrod into action.

"Let her go." He took a step forward, searching for anything that would pass for a weapon.

"Now where's the fun in that?" Luke raised the ice to her forehead and drew it across her hairline. Sullivan screamed. "Shall I carve off her face for you? A keepsake?"

"I'll do anything. Name it. Let her go."

"Anything?" Luke skimmed the knifelike shard of ice lower, past her temple, slicing slightly deeper.

She whimpered, blood running down her face.

"Here's the problem, Jarrod," he said. "We all saw what happened on the roof. I had your hand, if you'll recall, ready to snip off your fingers. But I hesitated, and things got messy." He looked down at Sullivan. "I learn from my mistakes."

The edge of the ice slid across her neck with a soft *slish*. Sullivan's eyes went wide. A split second passed, one fairy tale moment before the blood came. She parted her lips, a thick bubble of red rising from her. Her head rocked back a fraction of an inch, opening the split across her throat.

Luke dropped her and tossed the already melting ice.

"No!" Jarrod leaped, caught her in his arms before she hit the snow. "No, no," he moaned, ripping off his coat, trying to press it against the wound.

"No more hesitations," Luke said as he walked away, brushing his hands together. "Send Gabriel and Eden my fucking regards."

Sullivan choked. For a horrible second Jarrod thought she was trying to say his name, but it was only the blood.

So much blood. Running off her, down his legs, seeping into the snow, soaking his gloves.

"Don't die!" He yanked the gloves off, not caring about passing her Touch. His hands fluttered over her cheeks, her hair, and finally grabbed her hand, the fingers slick in his. He met her eyes, didn't look away even as life faded from her, her eyelids falling to half-mast.

"Sullivan," he whispered. He shifted her onto his lap, pulled her against him. In the dark night, the snow fell. Jarrod dropped his face against her coat, his cheek coated in the sticky gore that covered them both. Far off, he heard Luke laughing in the empty park.

He felt nothing. The sun was rising. His hand was frozen in hers somewhere under the foot of new-fallen snow, deep enough that it had hidden the blood. His breaths were slow, even. A shadow crossed in front of him, but Jarrod didn't look up. Let them find him—angel, mortal, Sider. He didn't care.

The shadow moved again. No one was yelling, no frantic phone calls to the police.

"Don't touch her," Jarrod said.

"I won't."

Jarrod raised his head slowly, his neck creaking. "Gabe," he said. Jarrod stared down at Sullivan's face, the only part of her he'd kept free of snow. "Luke. Luke, he . . . we were walking and he came out of nowhere and he . . ."

Gabe gripped his shoulder. "Jarrod, you have to let go of her, okay?"

He shook his head fiercely. "No. She's . . . I just . . ."

"It's been hours, Jarrod. I brought a blanket, and we're going to wrap her up in it and I'm going to carry her for you. We're going to take care of her together, okay?"

Gabe knelt and began to brush the snow away.

"I said don't touch her," Jarrod snapped, twisting away from him.

"We need to get her warm." Gabe moved down to uncover her legs. "Before she wakes up."

Jarrod's mouth opened, his breath stalling. "Wakes up?" he finally forced out.

Gabe nodded.

"No, that's impossible." Jarrod threw the snow off her, his fingers finding her neck, the skin there firm beneath his hands. He turned back to Gabe. "How?"

"Touch." Gabe dropped beside them, the snow blooming red where his knees pressed down into the frozen layer of blood. "She did too much. It ate her path away."

Pathless. But that would mean . . . Jarrod gave a half cry, grabbed for Sullivan's hand. "Is she one of us?"

The fingers in his squeezed.

Sullivan took a breath.

ACKNOWLEDGMENTS

Writing this book is one of the hardest things I've ever done. These are the people who got me through.

To Devyn Burton, whose phone calls and Just Because emails were the sanity I needed to get through some very dark days.

To Courtney Allison Moulton, for amazingness and laughs and road-trips and the company that every Misery needs.

To Victoria Schwab, for baked goods and uttering the exact words I needed to hear at the exact moment I needed to hear them. I'm not sure where this book would be if you hadn't been here that day, bb.

To Martha Mihalick, Virginia Duncan, Marisa Russell, and everyone else at Greenwillow and HarperCollins for their infinite patience and guidance. You guys make my life.

To Rosemary Stimola, who is my champion and the reason I got to put the last check on my List of Writing Dreams.

To Chelsea Swiggett and Emili Hofer, who never wavered in their excitement when I read them early chapters (out loud . . . often . . . before I would let them leave . . .). I promise no spoilers on the next one!

To Kulsuma Begum who gave Vaughn his name and saved my butt!

For being awesome from the start: Chas Lilly, Kayla Beck, Amber Sweeney, Kari Olson, Rachel Clarke, and so many bloggers and friends who have spread the word about my characters and loved and hated them as much as I do.

So many scenes and feelings in this novel would not exist without the songs that played while I wrote them. A huge thank you to Amanda Palmer, Nine Inch Nails, Fever Ray, Digital Daggers, The Kills, HIM, The Birthday Massacre, Florence and the Machine, Yeah Yeah Yeahs, Rasputina, Puscifer, Menomena, Lissie, Laura Marling, and The Pretty Reckless. You guys rock my imaginary world.